Ptolemy rubbed his head against each of them, and the female cats gently licked his ears. He had cared for each of them as they had been found and fostered by the old astronomer.

"Good-bye," he said softly. "You are going forth to fulfill a noble destiny. God be with you, and may He bring you safely home once again, after you have found the Messiah."

—from *Three Wise Cats*

THREE WISE CATS

A CHRISTMAS STORY

HAROLD M. KONSTANTELOS AND
TERRI JENKINS-BRADY

B

BERKLEY BOOKS
NEW YORK

THE BERKLEY PUBLISHING GROUP
Published by the Penguin Group
Penguin Group (USA) Inc.
375 Hudson Street, New York, New York 10014, USA

Penguin Group (Canada), 90 Eglinton Avenue East, Suite 700, Toronto, Ontario M4P 2Y3, Canada (a division of Pearson Penguin Canada Inc.) • Penguin Books Ltd., 80 Strand, London WC2R 0RL, England • Penguin Group Ireland, 25 St. Stephen's Green, Dublin 2, Ireland (a division of Penguin Books Ltd.) • Penguin Group (Australia), 250 Camberwell Road, Camberwell, Victoria 3124, Australia (a division of Pearson Australia Group Pty. Ltd.) • Penguin Books India Pvt. Ltd., 11 Community Centre, Panchsheel Park, New Delhi—110 017, India • Penguin Group (NZ), 67 Apollo Drive, Rosedale, Auckland 0632, New Zealand (a division of Pearson New Zealand Ltd.) • Penguin Books (South Africa) (Pty.) Ltd., 24 Sturdee Avenue, Rosebank, Johannesburg 2196, South Africa

Penguin Books Ltd., Registered Offices: 80 Strand, London WC2R 0RL, England

This is a work of fiction. Names, characters, places, and incidents either are the product of the authors' imagination or are used fictitiously, and any resemblance to actual persons, living or dead, business establishments, events, or locales is entirely coincidental. The publisher does not have any control over and does not assume any responsibility for author or third-party websites or their content.

PUBLISHING HISTORY
Write Up the Road edition / December 2005
Berkley hardcover edition / November 2009
Berkley trade paperback edition / November 2012

Berkley trade paperback ISBN: 978-0-425-26389-1

The Library of Congress has catalogued the Berkley hardcover as follows:

Konstantelos, Harold M.
Three wise cats : a Christmas story / Harold M. Konstantelos and Terri Jenkins-Brady.—
Berkley hardcover ed.
p. cm.
ISBN 978-0-425-23036-7 (alk. paper)
1. Cats—Fiction. 2. Christmas stories. I. Jenkins-Brady, Terri. II. Title.
PS3611.O59T47 2009
813'.6—dc22
2009028327

PRINTED IN THE UNITED STATES OF AMERICA

10 9 8 7 6 5 4 3 2 1

TO KIKI
WITH ALL MY LOVE,
HAROLD

TO TIM
MY ONE AND ONLY,
LOVE, TERRI

THREE WISE CATS

PTOLEMY HAD GAZED at the night sky from the window in the tower until his neck ached. There was indeed a star beginning to glow a bit brighter than its neighbors. He sighed and left the windowsill, seating himself on the hearth. Only a few fading coals still glowed. The last hours of the night were small indeed.

"There is no other way," he said softly to the dark room surrounding him. "But I do regret sending such young ones out into the world. There are many dangers that could befall them."  He thought for a minute of the three he would soon bid farewell: Kezia, the coquettish tabby, who could catch a mouse as quickly as one could blink; Abishag, who felt she could overcome any adversity after being orphaned at only four weeks; and Ira, youngest of the three and boldest because of his youth. They counted four scant years among them all. Whether that small amount of living experience would be sufficient for overcoming the inevitable mistakes and pitfalls upon a journey was yet to be seen.

He tucked his front paws under his chest and settled himself to wait for the other three cats. They would regard his news as a call to high adventure. But here in the astronomer's tower room, he would wait anxiously for their return. "If they return," he said slowly, as dawn slipped past the window, "they will bear news such as this earth has not yet seen."

"I DON'T SEE why you can't go, too," Kezia hissed, lashing her tail from side to side. She drew her small mouth into its cutest pout. That usually convinced even humans to do as she wished.

"All of us cannot go on this quest," Ptolemy said for the fourth or fifth time. "It would not fulfill the prophecy of *the three finding the one*, if I accompanied you. And—" He glanced at the elderly astronomer and religious scholar, dozing again amid a desktop clutter of papyrus rolls and parchment maps.

"I cannot leave him; his time grows shorter with each labored breath he draws. I do not know whether he has years or merely months left, but it would be cruel to leave him totally alone in this tower. At least I can meow and scratch at the housekeeper's door until someone hears me and brings us both water and something to eat."

Abishag got up on her sturdy legs and walked over to the chair in which the aged astronomer slumped.

"He looks very frail," she said, looking up at him. "He wouldn't last long at all if we tried to take him with us." And shaking her head, she went over to the bowl of water in the corner.

"That wouldn't fulfill the prophecy either," Ptolemy reminded her.

With a loud yowl, Ira uncoiled from another corner, where he had been nearly invisible, and leaped at Kezia.

"Stop that!" Kezia slapped at Ira with her paw. "I think we ought to leave you here and take Ptolemy with us, that's what I think. So there!"

Ira grinned at her. The effect was startling; he had such very white teeth and such very black fur.

"Nah," he answered, skipping nimbly away from Kezia's continued efforts to land a blow on his head. "We'll travel fast and we'll travel far. Our twelve legs all together aren't but a quarter as old as Mr. P. here."

The old cat shook his head, refusing to be baited or teased. "Know that you will be able to take nothing with you. Hunting will be your only means of provision, unless you meet some extraordinarily kind humans. Seeing Abishag at the water bowl reminds me: Once you get to the far desert lands, the water well belongs to the town. Visitors and strangers are forbidden to drink from the well."

"Then what must we do? Ask for water?" Abishag's cautious nature asserted itself. She was beginning to feel more worried than pleased at being asked to go on such a momentous journey.

"That would be the wisest course, I think," Ptolemy said and then leaned close to her and rubbed his head against hers. "Don't worry. Your two companions have been carefully chosen also, and the three of you will somehow surmount all obstacles." She sighed, gathered her paws underneath her, and settled back onto the cold flagstone floor.

"I'm listening. Please go on, Ptolemy."

"You will be on your journey a very long time," Ptolemy began. "I believe you may travel for a longer period than even I did as a small kitten. I left my home in the Far East as a gift from the powerful Muang king to our astronomer, who had saved the king's life by foretelling great danger. We were traveling the desert silk route with a small army to protect us on our way to Alexandria—"

"What!" squeaked Kezia. "You've been in the presence of kings, seen palaces and great fortunes, and done all this traveling yourself, and you never told us any of this?"

Ptolemy frowned and continued. "A band of brigands—cutthroats, the worst thieves in the known world—set upon us in spite of the armed men riding on all sides. Had I not been hidden by the astronomer in the sleeve of his robe, I should have been taken as a rarity and sold for a small fortune, for many men had never seen a cat of my markings before in their lives.

"Anyway, we obviously did get to Alexandria, and sailed from that huge port here to Lepcis Magna, on the coast of the Mediterranean Sea, part of the new Roman province of Africa. As astronomers and scholars, we serve the Roman Empire at Augustus Caesar's pleasure.

"You will actually be retracing part of my journey during yours, so perhaps some of my earlier experiences will aid you. Before you set out in three weeks, I will relate to you anything at all which may help you."

Kezia was still staring at him. "I know the astronomer named all of us, choosing our names from one of his religious texts. But where did he get your odd name?"

"Our astronomer named me for Ptolemy Philadelphus, the pharaoh of Egypt who founded the Alexandria library. How I wish I could have visited it myself!"

The tabby laid her head down, put her dainty paws over her ears, and refused to look at Ptolemy.

Abishag nudged her. "What's wrong? Why are you pouting again?"

"He could have told us at least a little of this before," Kezia whispered, her injured feelings very apparent. "I might have been given as a gift to a king or someone of royal blood myself, if only I'd known he had all these connections." And she sniffled slightly.

Ptolemy smiled under his whiskers. He'd heard the whispers. And that was one reason he'd never told the charming but rather vain little cat his past. *She will see the King of Kings, the Messiah,* he thought. *What greater gift could exist than that?*

Behind a loose stone at the corner of the fireplace crouched Asmodeus, a rat none of the four cats had been able to catch and kill. He was almost as big as Ira and nearly as well educated as Ptolemy. Abishag had caught him once, as Asmodeus did lack her stoic patience—but he had gotten away, leaving only a tuft of fur and a piece of skin in her teeth.

Well, well, Asmodeus thought, licking his greasy lips. *So they're departing for adventure? That morsel of bacon was delicious, but far from ample for a meal. And tough, also, particularly since I lack the means for adequate chewing. I deserve far better than this. I believe I shall accompany them. Whatever booty they manage to get should be mine as well as theirs.*

He carefully curled his tail, broken so many times in so many fights, over his back and slipped behind another stone to be closer to the soft murmurs as the cats conversed. With only one good eye, he had to check carefully in the dim light to be sure Ptolemy wasn't watching for him. He snickered to himself. *Mr. Philosopher will certainly be angered when he finds I've journeyed with them. He thinks I am evil, sure to bring them to ruin by my mere association. Bah! What the gods will to happen, happens. I have no part in that. But I will watch over his darlings constantly, indeed, as carefully as if they were my own little precious ratlings.*

Ptolemy lifted his head and sniffed. "I smell rat," he told the other three cats. "Asmodeus is listening. Be wary of him; he may try to frighten you by telling you tales, perhaps of humans who paint their faces blue and eat cats for dinner."

Ira yawned. "They'll have to catch us first."

"They also do not do such things," Ptolemy continued. "They are called Tauregs; desert dwellers and nomads, they may be rough and uncivilized but they do not eat cats. They may"—he raised his voice so the listener in the shadows would hear him—"catch and eat rats, for they do not tolerate useless creatures who try to live in their tents."

A scurrying sound to one side of the fireplace made Ptolemy grin widely, and he nodded at Abishag. She laughed, knowing full well who'd made the noises, and washed her face with her paw.

THEIR LESSONS COMMENCED in earnest the next day. Since the elderly astronomer's maps were only those of the heavens, Ptolemy taught the younger cats how to keep their course by the stars, and the land features to keep in mind. Fortunately, their astronomer's tower lay at the outskirts of Lepcis Magna, so their first week's travel on the road should see them within the city. Once there in the Roman Empire's outpost, they would eat well: rats and mice abounded, and they might even be lucky enough to beg some cream or butter, to start a small layer of fat beneath their fur coats.

"Keep in mind that even though the days are so warm you should drink water as often as possible, you must begin to prepare for the much colder days and nights ahead. The seasons are changing, and you must also, to survive." The aged Siamese stopped and looked at his three charges. Kezia was dozing in the warm sunlight; Abishag was busy trying to sniff out a mouse, which had hidden itself in the wall around the water well; and Ira was yawning while carefully examining each claw.

"Go on, old man," he said to Ptolemy. "I'm listening. You and I both know it will be me who does the fighting and the exploring. The ladies aren't up to it."

Abishag crept up behind him and boxed an ear. "I'm a better hunter than you are any day!" The two leaped at each other then and rolled across the dirt of the courtyard as a black bundle of hisses and paw swipes. Ptolemy lay down, nudging Kezia over so he got a share of the sunshine, too.

"I may as well end the lessons for today," he said above the growls and muffled threats.

Kezia stirred. "I was listening. I heard everything you said." She yawned and pushed her paws into his thick fur, warming them.

The much bigger cat sighed. "I most truly hope so."

Asmodeus slipped across the top of the wall that separated the tower's courtyard from the open area leading to the gate. *I hope so, too. Their studies are not proceeding well, obviously. Once out in the world, if they don't keep their tiny wits about them, they shall all be killed. But then, they are not my responsibility. Journey I shall, for it is far too dreary and predictable in this tower to suit my cultured tastes.*

Soon the short time they had left to spend in the tower

was gone, and dawn on the day of their departure came in a glorious haze of gold, peach, and palest blue.

Ptolemy went to find Ira; Abishag and Kezia were already sitting in the courtyard, sniffing the cool air and eager to be off.

Ira had a paw firmly planted on Asmodeus's head as Ptolemy hurried into the tower room where they had all lived. "Be careful!" he called to the younger cat. "Remember, a rat's bite is often fatal, because of the vileness of his mouth." Ira lazily lifted his paw and let Asmodeus escape, screaming curses at the cat as he fled.

"I could've had him for breakfast," Ira explained, "but he smelled too bad to eat."

Ptolemy chuckled. "Come on, Ira the Hunter. The girls are ready to depart."

He rubbed his head against each of them, and the female cats gently licked his ears. He had cared for each of them as they had been found and fostered by the old astronomer.

"Good-bye," he said softly. "You are going forth to fulfill a noble destiny. God be with you, and may He bring you safely home once again, after you have found the Messiah."

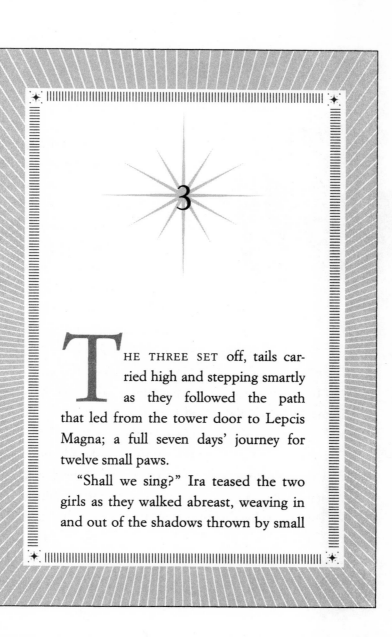

3

THE THREE SET off, tails carried high and stepping smartly as they followed the path that led from the tower door to Lepcis Magna; a full seven days' journey for twelve small paws.

"Shall we sing?" Ira teased the two girls as they walked abreast, weaving in and out of the shadows thrown by small bushes growing wild beside the same path humans used.

"What are you mewling about?" Abishag asked absently. She was more interested in watching for a tasty snack of a few butterflies or a beetle than what her foster brother had to say. While they'd eaten a very good breakfast—Ptolemy had stayed up half the night to catch each of them three plump, tender mice—she still could always manage a mouthful of dessert. And hadn't he said they needed to put fat on their bones?

"If we sing, we'll attract attention, once we have humans about," Kezia said sternly. "And Ptolemy said to be as inobstru—unobtu—invisible as possible."

Ira laughed; he felt in his heart this was the adventure to which he'd been born. And so as he walked, he purred to himself, enjoying the day and the warming sunshine.

They slept that night burrowed into a small haystack not far from the path, which had now widened to a road as they neared a village.

"I still wish Ptolemy had come with us." Abishag yawned as she snuggled closer to Kezia.

"We could all use his thick fur coat and warm paws about now," Kezia answered.

"This is nothing!" Ira boasted. "When he took me along for the falcon hunt last winter, it was far colder than this at night. And I, still a kitten, slept by myself."

"Then you can do so again," Kezia said, and she pushed him away from where the two girls were curled up in the fragrant dried hay.

"Oh, well." He sighed. "I'll take the first watch."

"First watch?" Abishag asked.

"I intend to make this trip into a soldier's campaign. And soldiers stand watches."

"Why?"

"To make sure enemies don't slip up on us."

"Are you speaking of fierce dogs?"

Ira grinned in the dim light from the setting moon. "Dogs, owls, snakes, humans with brooms . . ."

"Will you two please quit talking so I can get some sleep!" Kezia hissed.

"Yes, ma'am." Ira winked at Abishag

and slipped behind the haystack. He climbed to the top of it, curled his long tail about himself, and settled in to watch.

Three hours later, he leaped to his feet when something touched him on his back.

"Who's there!" he demanded and heard his foster sister laugh.

"Just me, Abishag." She giggled and climbed up beside him. "Go get some sleep, Ira the Soldier. I think this sentry plan is a good idea. I'll watch until dawn for you."

"But that's two watches," Ira objected.

"Well, we'll have to stay hidden tomorrow once we're in the town anyway, so I may as well sleep then," Abishag said practically. "And Kezia is truly tired, so let her sleep tonight. She'll take her turn, too, once she realizes it's the best way for us to be safe."

"Well, then, good night." Ira climbed back down the haystack and curled up a few inches from Kezia; he was sound asleep almost before he completed a quick bath.

Abishag stared up at the stars, frowning, until she located the North Star as Ptolemy had taught her to do.

So I keep my nose pointed to that and we'll find Lepcis Magna. I do wish Ptolemy had decided to come along with us. I miss him already, and we've only been gone a day. I hope the old astronomer doesn't die before we return. No one will look after Ptolemy at all then.

Dawn came, and Abishag stretched several times and licked a few stray hairs into place before picking her way down the haystack to where the other two still slept. Resisting the impulse to leap upon them and startle them awake, she patted Kezia with a paw.

"Wake up, Kezia; it's morning and we need to get hunting."

The tabby stretched and yawned, then nudged Ira.

"Wake up, lazy one. We need to begin traveling again."

After a quick breakfast of several foolishly inquisitive quail, they washed up and set out once more.

"My paws are sore," Kezia said, worried. "I thought they would get tougher as we walked farther and farther."

"Try resting them by walking alongside the road, in the grass," Ira suggested. "And once we're in the village, we'll slip into someone's barn and see if we can't beg some cream to put on all our paws."

Kezia brightened at the thought and kept trudging on, veering into the grassy places as she found them.

Off to the side of the road and running in a ditch worn by a small trickle of water, Asmodeus kept pace with the cats, grumbling to himself. *Tsk, tsk. I should never have set out on this journey. What was I thinking of, to join this foolishness? Did I not have sufficient provisions to steal and enjoy back at the tower? Oh, my poor feet—they are throbbing and swelling so. It's all their fault, dratted cats. If they hadn't enticed me with*

their dreams of glory and descriptions of feasts so real it made my mouth water, I wouldn't be here now.

The next days passed fairly uneventfully; the resourceful cats managed several times to put fresh cream on their paws, and then as they kept walking, gradually the pads became tougher. The three grew used to being outside and to relying upon each other. They were together now, for ill or for good, a small band of comrades set out upon a grand adventure.

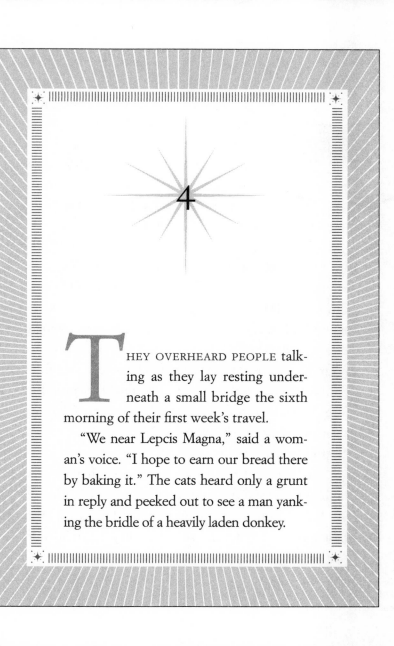

4

THEY OVERHEARD PEOPLE talking as they lay resting underneath a small bridge the sixth morning of their first week's travel.

"We near Lepcis Magna," said a woman's voice. "I hope to earn our bread there by baking it." The cats heard only a grunt in reply and peeked out to see a man yanking the bridle of a heavily laden donkey.

"Move, you filthy beast!" He slapped the animal on its hindquarters, but it refused to move.

Two extremely dirty little girls caught sight of the cats and made a squealing, excited dash straight for them. Kezia raced toward a rabbit's burrow; Abishag scurried under a tree root; and Ira leaped behind the stone bridge support. The girls scrambled about on the dry creek's banks and stones, driving Ira from his first hiding place and under some thorny bushes. Their mother screamed at them, threatening dire punishments if they didn't rejoin their parents promptly. Finally the girls, arms and faces scratched from the bushes, gave up trying to catch the black male cat. They had turned back to the road, reluctantly following their parents, when the youngest shrieked:

"Oooh, a rat, a disgusting rat!"

"See, Mater? That's why we need a cat for our new home," the oldest daughter whined.

"We need no cat," their father groused. "Leave it. And hasten yourselves, for this stupid donkey has decided to trot once again, and I will not halt it."

Once the family was out of sight, the three cats crept out from their hiding places and met on the now-empty road. They touched noses. "That was a close call," Kezia said. "And what was that about a rat?"

Ira was sniffing the air. "I think we may have company. That stink is too familiar."

"What's that noise?" Abishag turned quickly and looked down the road. "I've never heard anything like that before."

An odd thumping, a jingle, and other sounds they couldn't identify were moving toward them.

"I think we'd better hide again," Kezia said, and she fled back to the rabbit's burrow she'd found so fortuitously.

Abishag raced up the same tree whose root had sheltered her and sat on a branch close to the trunk, her black fur seeming to be part of the rough bark.

Ira, fascinated by all the many noises, still sat in the road, turning his head, his upper lip flehmening.

"Get out of the road!" Abishag hissed at him.

Just then, a creature bigger than any of them had ever seen in their lives appeared. Whatever it was, it had fur and four legs—but it was far too huge to be any sort of a cat, or even the largest of dogs. It dragged some contrivance behind it that glittered in the sun—with a human standing inside. Ira stared until his ears hurt because his eyes were open so wide.

A sudden rustling sound behind him, and Asmodeus streaked across the roadway and right under the nose of the creature. First it snorted and then it screamed. It suddenly stood on its hind legs, making odd moaning noises and striking out with its front paws. The human cursed and pulled at some ropes the creature had tied to its fur, while the thing it dragged tilted and nearly fell. Frightened, Ira lost his wits for a moment and cowered as the huge beast staggered closer and closer to him. Abishag began scrambling back down the tree.

Kezia ran out from the burrow just in time to see the huge creature standing and trembling with all four paws back on the road's surface—and Ira lying in the dirt. With a cry, she ran to the black cat's body. Abishag joined her and they began calling their foster brother's name, frantically pawing at him and licking his face.

"What kind of a warhorse are you, you fool?" Lavines Gracus shouted at the creature. "The gods would not have you for a pack animal! You enter battles bravely enough and yet nearly kill me because of an outsized mouse!" He called to his servant, Citus, who had scrambled from the chariot when it first began to sway. "Take the reins!"

He stepped down from the chariot and took off his helmet, running a hand through the thick hair beneath it. He glanced at his *centuria*, his company of soldiers who had halted, still in formation, when they saw their commander's horse panic.

Kezia and Abishag were too worried to notice anything going on around them, still trying to determine if Ira lived.

Ira finally roused himself, protesting, "Stop it, girls, you're going to lick off my eyebrows." Then he moaned softly. "Ow, that hurts. I feel sick . . ."

"What's wrong? Where are you hurt?" Abishag stopped licking his face and stepped back to get a good look at him. His left front leg was at an odd angle.

Just then, the Roman centurion turned and saw the three cats beside the road. His face paled.

"By Mars's shield," he said breathlessly. "My dream—it must

be an omen from the gods." He pointed to the group of cats with one hand and motioned his servant over with the other. "I dreamed about these three just last night. Two black cats and one striped tabby." He frowned. "But none of them were injured. I hope I have not offended any of the gods, so that they take their favor from me."

Gracus approached the cats quietly, speaking in a soft voice. "All is well, little ones. I dreamed about you; you were meant to be on this road today. And I hope I may assist you so that the gods will look favorably upon me."

Kezia and Abishag eyed each other. "Should we run?" Abishag asked.

"Run in different directions," Ira advised. "That way he can't catch both of you. And I'll bite him if he comes near me, so you may then escape." And he laid his head

back on his right paw; his other front leg hurt too badly even to share the weight of his small head.

The centurion dropped to one knee, looking at Ira. "My horse has broken this small one's leg," he observed, noting the hoofprints in the dirt. "If the ground had not been soft, the limb surely would have been severed. And yet he bears the pain without complaint. He must be a small soldier himself."

At that compliment, Ira's eyes opened and he tried to purr. Gracus heard him. "He answers me! Bring my shield!" he called to Citus.

Carefully the two men picked up the small black cat, using the shield as a stretcher. "Pitch the tents beside the road," the centurion commanded. "We camp here tonight. Lepcis Magna and our garrison must wait until this small one has had his injuries tended." He turned toward the two other cats, who were fidgeting nervously as they saw their foster brother about to be taken away. "Come, you must stay together as I dreamed of you," he told them gently. "I will bind your brother's wounds and care for him in a manner befitting a soldier. And you two shall also come with us."

He set Ira's broken leg, roughly but not unkindly, washed the blood away from his cuts where the hooves had nicked him, and then gave him a tiny drop of something to make him sleep. Once his tent was up, he fed the other two cats and told Citus to find a large basket among the supplies.

When the servant returned, Gracus took a rough wool cloak and placed it and Ira in the basket. "Sleep well, little ones," he told Kezia and Abishag. "Watch over your brother if you wish, but my heart tells me he will be all right. I have set his broken leg, and if the gods will it, he shall run and play with you once more. I will hang a sling of leather in my chariot, so he may be carried in a few days and not try to hobble on three legs. And you two may ride in my chariot also, either in your basket or at my feet. You shall all three arrive in Lepcis Magna in a manner befitting those chosen by the gods!"

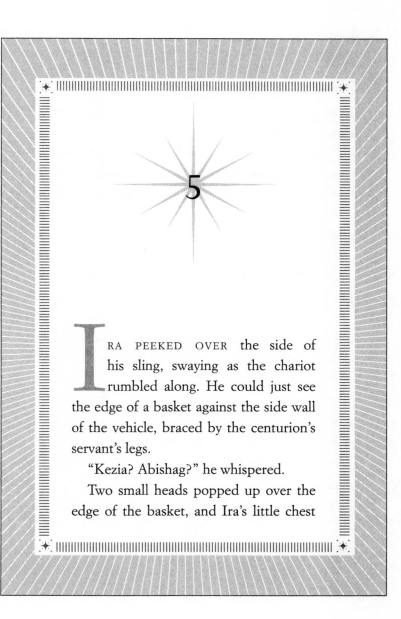

5

IRA PEEKED OVER the side of his sling, swaying as the chariot rumbled along. He could just see the edge of a basket against the side wall of the vehicle, braced by the centurion's servant's legs.

"Kezia? Abishag?" he whispered.

Two small heads popped up over the edge of the basket, and Ira's little chest heaved a tremendous sigh. Although he wouldn't admit it, he felt much braver when he was with the other two cats. "What happened?"

"Don't you remember?" Kezia hissed. "That peculiar creature that broke your leg is called a *horse*."

"You could have been killed," Abishag added. "Gracus looked after you; he said you were a little soldier."

Ira smiled. "And so I am. I told you I was going to be a soldier this trip. Ptolemy knew what he was doing, to send me with you two," he began bragging.

"Oh, hush," Kezia replied. "Thanks to you, I'm not seeing Lepcis Magna. We're going around the city and to the garrison on the outskirts. I wanted to see ladies in rich, fine dresses and jewels and—"

"The best thing about it is that we're riding instead of walking," Abishag interrupted. "I wouldn't want to walk through these crowds. And to go around all the people and then down to the harbor would take us another week."

The servant, Citus, hearing the whispering and hissing noises, reached down and clumsily patted both girls on their heads. "We are soon at quarters, small ones."

Gracus, guiding the nervous horse and his chariot through a stream of pushing, shoving people, paid no attention as he kept a firm hold on the reins.

They reached the garrison and the servant jumped out of the chariot, taking the horse by its bridle and holding it as Gracus put Ira's sling over his shoulder and picked up the basket. "Come, you will stay in my quarters while we await our new orders," he told them. He set the basket down and laid the sling on the floor.

"Now you must learn to walk again, but continue to favor that leg until it heals," he advised Ira, who stood and briskly shook himself. He looked up at Gracus and purred very loudly, and the centurion's stern, weathered face softened into a smile.

"Indeed you are welcome," he said and turned to go out the door. His servant was already bringing in the small bag of Gracus's belongings. "Feed them, and let them explore the post," he told the man. "I must report to my *legatus*, my commander."

Kezia was struggling to climb out of the basket, and Citus turned it on its side so she and Abishag could get out easily. Then he set the basket and its wool cloak near the cot on which Gracus would sleep. He left for a few minutes, then returned with a full bucket of water and set it down next to a rough table. Rummaging in a small bundle, he pulled out a short tallow candle in a holder and placed it on the tabletop.

"He lives as his men do, in a sparing manner," he told the three cats, who were watching him intently. "Now I'll go ask the cook for some scraps for you."

An hour later, they wandered about the garrison, searching out the sources of different smells and reminding Ira to keep walking, to strengthen his leg as it healed.

"It still hurts if I put much weight on it, and it itches under the wrappings," he told his foster sisters. "But at least it's not throbbing like it did."

Back in Gracus's room, Asmodeus was chewing at the candle and again grumbling to himself. *This is very poor fare. Did they think to save even the smallest portion, or even crumbs perhaps, for poor Asmodeus? No, certainly not. They dined well, with never a thought of gratitude for me. But who procured for them their transport all the way through the city, I ask? They would have spent at least*

*a week just wandering, if they hadn't ridden in a grand
chariot. While I, who have digested more parchments than
they could ever have read to them, arrived in a supply
wagon. A supply wagon, for such as I!*

The rat devoured the leather thongs that had bound
Gracus's bag and then looked about the sparsely
furnished room for anything else on which to nibble.
He jumped down from the tabletop and crept along
the wall toward the open door. "I shall have to find the
cook," he muttered and slipped through the door.

That evening, Gracus returned and tried to light the
candle with a flint. Failing that, he sent Citus to the
supply clerk for a new one, then turned to
the three cats when the bright flame lit the
remains of the old candle.

"A rat!" Gracus's voice was disgusted.
"Even sent by the gods, you cats surely must
know how to rid my quarters of vermin. See
that you do so."

The centurion unrolled and studied a
small map for a short time, then blew out the
candle flame and went to bed. Citus slept in
the corner, curled up in another cloak.

A whispered conference took place in the dim moonlight coming through the window.

"Gracus sounded angry. We must catch that rat," Abishag said. "If we don't, we may have to find our own way to the far desert, without any more help."

"What do you mean?" Kezia asked. "Surely Gracus wouldn't turn us out to be on our own now."

"It's Asmodeus's fault," Ira said emphatically. "He ate the candle and the leather thongs; I can tell by the smell. He's somehow followed us here. First, what we need to do is get rid of any other vermin in the compound. Then we can figure out a plot to catch Asmodeus. Remember, even Ptolemy said he's wily. I should never have turned that rat loose. I'd caught him sleeping, the morning we left."

"I nearly had him also," Abishag reminded her foster brother. "The bit of skin and fur I took off of him tasted as horrible as he smells."

"Just watch me catch him," Kezia said smugly. "He won't get away from *me*. I'll kill him and save his tail for a collar."

The next morning Gracus set his bare feet upon the floor, jumped, and then began chuckling. He laughed until his servant rushed in with a bucket of fresh water.

"What has happened?"

Gracus pointed, gasping for breath. On the floor were three neat rows of assorted-sized rats and mice—and a very large black beetle.

The centurion wiped his face with the back of his hand.

"I have not enjoyed a laugh like that in years. The three must have been sent by Mars! They do valiant battle with vermin. But I do not wish their gifts to be my breakfast. Where are they?"

Citus smiled. "They are asleep in their basket, sir. They must have hunted all night, as you bade them. I did not know there were so many parasites within these walls." He got a rush broom from beside the door and began gingerly sweeping the carcasses into a heap. "What shall I do with them?"

"Cast them onto the refuse pile outside. Perhaps the other repulsive creatures will see the remains and shun at least my quarters. And see if you may beg some butter or cream from the cook. They deserve to be richly rewarded for their long night's work."

6

KEZIA'S DAINTY PAW had Asmodeus pinned by his broken ruin of a tail and hind legs. With her other paw upraised, she hesitated, not quite sure where to land a death blow on the rat's thick neck.

Asmodeus squirmed and pleaded, trying to twist or talk himself free. "Let me go, sweet kitten," he pleaded. "Beautiful one, let me run and I'll . . . I'll bring you something as pretty . . . no, *nearly* as pretty . . . as yourself." He smiled over his broken tooth.

Kezia shuddered, he looked so awful. "Do hush," she said, turning her head slightly. She was looking for help. "I'm not listening to anything you have to say." *Where is Abishag? She's killed more rats than I have. How hard do I strike him? And where, exactly?*

"But it's jewelry," Asmodeus said. "Jewels to match your eyes." *I've heard human males say that to females. Let us see if it works on conceited cats.*

The young cat turned toward him again. "What about my eyes?"

"They are akin to grand jewels, lovely one. Wouldn't you desire something that would make them sparkle like a star?"

Kezia put her entire weight on her paw, keeping Asmodeus pinned to the dirt floor of the storehouse.

"You're lying."

"No, I assure you I am not."

"Yes, you must be. You're a liar and a thief. You've been

eating the grain and other foodstuffs stored in the compound. What you don't eat, you ruin with your nasty castings." Kezia drew back her other paw again.

"Stay your paw! I shall bring you a bracelet of topaz stones. It belongs to one of the camp followers and she will not dare to say it is missing," Asmodeus insisted.

"What would I do with a woman's bracelet? And what is a camp follower?"

"You have led far too sheltered a life; but that does not concern me now. You are so fine boned, do you not realize a woman's bracelet would easily clasp about your neck, to serve as a collar fit for a queen?"

"Fine boned?" Kezia tilted her head. "Well—I am, compared to Abishag, at least." She giggled. "Abishag's legs look like mushroom stems, or little stumps."

Asmodeus saw his escape dawning. "Exactly. Some-one of your refinement deserves jewelry for her neck, to set off her richly colored fur. Show the world what a fine lady cat you are."

"What are topaz stones?"

"They have the same golden hints and hues within their depths as your own eyes, my beautiful young cat. Everyone would remark on the resemblance."

Asmodeus finished talking and lay quietly, watching Kezia think.

"But wouldn't that also be stealing?"

"Not from a detested camp follower, foolish one. They're wicked, lewd women. No one regards them with anything more than a sneer."

"Do you promise not to destroy any more grain?" she asked the rat sternly, shifting her weight again.

"Cease the ponderous movements of your feet." Asmodeus grunted. "Your true aggregate weight is cloaked by your fur."

"What?"

"I'll cease dining on Roman grain," he said, keeping his good eye trained on a knothole in the wooden wall of the granary. *I believe that will serve my purpose. I can surely contort myself enough to squeeze through that opening.*

Kezia sighed. *The bracelet sounds so pretty; I've never had pretty things. Ptolemy always said they would only make me vain, but just this one time I should like to appear as a fine lady cat.* "If I let you go, will you—will you bring me the bracelet?"

"Yes!" Asmodeus leaped free of Kezia's paw and dashed for the knothole before she changed her mind.

"I'll bring it to you tonight," he called back through the knothole, smirking at the tabby. "And you may reward me with a kiss." He laughed crudely and vanished.

Kezia shivered and went to find water in which to wash her paw. It stunk so of Asmodeus, she didn't want to put her tongue on it to wash it.

Very late that night, Kezia slipped out of Gracus's quarters, leaving Ira and Abishag asleep in their basket. She had lain awake, excitedly trying to picture in her mind the promised topaz stones. *But he's not coming,* she told herself after half an hour had passed. The only sound was the sentinel, walking his regular round inside the barricaded walls. *I let him go because of his promise and he's made a fool of me. I hope the others never find out that I had him pinned and yet let him go.*

Just then she heard a muted clinking sound to her left. Emerging from the shadows was the large rat, dragging something that glittered as the last rays of the setting moon struck it.

Kezia ran to Asmodeus, meeting him in the middle of the hard-packed dirt in front of the legionnaires' barracks.

"Asmodeus! You brought my bracelet! I mean—you brought my collar!"

"Quiet!" he snapped. "I risked my life to bring this bauble to you, and you announce it to the entire barracks? Where are your wits? Have you none?"

Kezia narrowed her eyes. "I could catch you again— and not turn you loose this time," she threatened.

"Nonsense," Asmodeus muttered, tugging at the clasp with his broken tooth and forepaws. "There—I have the clasp open. Turn your back to me and I shall fasten it about your neck."

A cold fear fluttered in Kezia's stomach. "No, you may fasten it under my chin, while you stand between my paws," she told him. She stepped in front of the rat. "Now you can't bite me and sever my spinal cord from behind. If you try to put an end to me by biting my throat, my claws will still mortally wound you even as I die."

For a long moment they faced each other. Asmodeus weighed his odds. *I had no idea she was that intelligent. She can add up facts and infer plans from them. Hmm. Well, let her have her silly treasure. I can yet turn this situation to my advantage.*

Standing on his hind feet, he pushed one end of the bracelet over the back of Kezia's neck, then bent under her throat and pulled the clasp and ring of the bracelet together. As he bit the clasp to close it, he snarled, "There! Are you satisfied, you conceited little harpy?" And Asmodeus scuttled into the shadows once again.

Ignorant of what a harpy was, Kezia raised her head high. *My, it's heavy. It must be real gold! I will look at myself in the puddles by the stream once the sun comes up.*

A few short hours later, Kezia was admiring herself in a wide puddle by the little stream that flowed through the permanent Roman camp. *He told the truth. My eyes do match the topaz stones.* She leaned farther over the puddle. *I hope he fastened the clasp completely. I wouldn't want to— Oh! The mud! The mud's slick because of the stream!* With cries rendered inaudible by the splash that followed them, Kezia fell headfirst into the swiftly flowing water. She tried to fight her way up to the surface, flailing her paws and choking on the water rushing into her mouth and nose during her futile efforts to yowl for help. *I'm going to drown! No one knows where I am. They will only find my body after I'm dead!*

Suddenly a sharp jerk on the bracelet stopped her tumble downstream, and she glimpsed Abishag's sturdy little legs through the swirls of water and foaming bubbles.

Abishag's mouth hurt, and her neck and shoulders ached from the strain of holding Kezia's body against the force of the water. *Oh, my, Kezia's heavy. I don't know if I can hold her for long—I can't pull her to the bank as I thought I could. And what has she around her neck? I tried to catch her by the scruff—but something metallic tasting is in the way. What do I do?* Then, with joy, she heard Citus running behind her, his sandals slapping the ground. Strong arms reached over her head and the servant's hands grasped the tabby cat.

Abishag turned loose her hold on Kezia and half swam, half waded over to the bank. Citus pulled Kezia into his arms, then turned her upside down and slapped her back. Kezia coughed, and a small amount of water ran out her nose and mouth. More water streamed from her fur after Citus set her back on the ground. "There, young one. The gods have smiled upon you and misfortune has not taken you early to meet them!"

Abishag touched her nose to Kezia's. "How did you fall into the stream?" The tabby cat's fur was so wet and matted, Abishag failed to see the heavy gold and topaz bracelet around her neck. Kezia shook herself hard, soaking her first rescuer's fur. Then the little black cat saw the gleam of jewels. "That's what I caught in my mouth! Where did you get that beautiful collar?"

"None of your business!" Kezia hissed, and she ran as fast as her wobbly legs would carry her to a patch of grass and sunlight, where she licked herself dry and into contentment once again.

When the several companies assembled for their midday meal, Kezia proudly walked along the line of strong legs, brushing against the men she favored and arching her back to be patted. Most of the soldiers made admiring comments, telling the tabby how fine she looked in her new collar. She preened and strutted until she wound herself around the camp commander's ankles—and was seized by hands that felt like bands of metal.

"Why is this creature wearing my Polla's bracelet?" The legatus's voice bellowed the question not two inches from Kezia's ears. She wiggled and tried to escape his grasp, but he held her by the scruff of her neck until she quit struggling and hung limply from his hand.

GRACUS HAD NO idea why he had been summoned from his meal to the commander's private quarters. But the uneasy feeling within his chest grew as he hurried through the open door and saw his tabby cat, crouched in a leather box with the lid partly covering the opening.

"What is wrong, Legatus?" The commander's slave woman, Polla, silently stood behind her master's chair.

"Why is your cat—for I am told it is your cat—wearing my slave's bracelet about its neck? Is it a tasteless prank?"

Inwardly Gracus sighed. No matter if someone in his company's ranks had done this as a joke, it still had fallen upon his head. "I do not know, sir. If you would permit me, I will remove the bracelet and return it to its rightful owner at once. And I shall question my men."

The commander raised one eyebrow and his patrician upper lip in a sneer. "You have not placed her bracelet upon the animal?"

"No, sir. I had not even heard of the thoughtless prank until this moment."

The slave Polla, beautiful and tall, whose thick blond braid hung down her back, hesitantly stepped forward and stood at her master's side.

"I am one who did this—prank?—you speak of," her voice was guttural, her Latin rough and uneducated.

The commander twisted his head to stare up at her. "Why? Did you think I give you baubles as playthings for vermin catchers? Or that the bracelet, which cost me three hundred sesterces, was worthless?"

"No, master. I grieve for my home. There I had cat, since I was little girl; young. I put bracelet on cat and admire cat; cat run away. It was a stupid thing. I am sorry."

The commander returned his stare to Gracus. "Obviously all women are foolish beings, who think only of playing and gossiping. Gracus, strip that cat of the bracelet and I will hear no more of this." He stood and strode from the room.

Without a word, Gracus stepped to the leather box and extricated Kezia. He removed the bracelet roughly and dropped it onto the commander's chair. He cast only one look at Polla from under his eyebrows as he turned to leave the room, a drooping Kezia under his arm, but was startled by her composure and her beauty.

"Thank you," he said awkwardly, unsure as to her motive for such an action—and such a lie. For he knew she was not telling the truth. He stalked out of the room, inexplicably angry with himself and with Polla. *Surely she will be beaten. Why did she tell such a lie? Was she attempting to protect the cat, or me? She is so very beautiful—perhaps—perhaps if the commander tires of her, as he has tired of so many other women before, I may purchase her. Her speech is untutored and harsh to the ears. But Citus could easily remedy that. And it would be pleasant to return to my tent when we are on a campaign and have her waiting there.*

7

A WEEK LATER, Gracus went to the stables to see about his chariot horse. It was still early in the morning, and Polla stood in the doorway to the commander's quarters. She looked at the centurion and dropped her head, watching him from under her lashes. He stopped and waited until she raised her head again.

"My servant related to me a most amazing tale," he began and stepped a few paces closer. *She is beautiful; only see her eyes. I wonder how much the legatus paid for her. Would she go with me willingly?*

"My foolish cat was punished for her theft, for she nearly drowned in the stream while wearing your beautiful bracelet. My servant rescued her by plucking her from the current. But what renders the story amazing—he swore to me her sister cat was trying to keep the tabby from being swept downstream."

She drew her eyebrows together, concentrating on his words. "I understand you. That one cat tried to hold fast the other?"

"So Citus insists."

She smiled at him. "They is—are—remarkable creatures, cats. I think they much kinder than humans eventimes."

He was a little puzzled. "Do you mean sometimes?"

"That must be the word, yes." She turned to go inside, and Gracus's eyes narrowed as he saw thin scabs from the whipping she had received still evident upon the backs of her arms. *The skin on her back must be torn to shreds. The legatus was too harsh with her.*

She cleared her throat. "Is it you will permit me to enjoy your cats—sometimes?"

"Do you mean you wish to play with them?"

"Please, yes."

"Certainly you may do so. I would gladly give you one of them, but they are seldom apart. And as I dreamed of them traveling together, I fear the gods might be angry if I separated them."

She nodded and left the doorway. Gracus resumed walking toward the stables, his mind no longer on his horse.

A few weeks later, the summer days and nights differed only by a few degrees' temperature from one another, and the cats sought the shade of the trees. Polla whiled away the hot hours by playing with the young cats.

Abishag lay a little apart from the others in the shade. Washing a front paw, she was trying not to think about how overly warm she was when she heard a voice call her name.

"Abishag, my young feline," the voice began. She lifted her nose and sniffed, then scowled.

"Asmodeus—phew! It has to be you—no one else stinks as badly as you do. What do you want?"

"No need to be rude, my dear cat," Asmodeus cautioned and moved toward her slightly. "I merely wanted to inquire as to your future plans."

"Future plans?"

"Well, you seem to be dallying here at the garrison quarters such a long time. Are you not supposed to be traveling in search of the Messiah?"

Abishag's eyes grew round as she gasped, "What do you know of our mission to find the Messiah?"

The rat sat upon his haunches and picked up his tail with one paw, smoothing and caressing it with the other.

"I know everything, my kitten. You must remember I heard you and the old cat, whispering and planning secretly while the others slept, unknowing and unworried."

"What do you mean? We had no secret plans."

Asmodeus snickered. "No? You did not tell them of the hunger, the bad weather, and the dangers they would be facing, did you? Nor did you tell them they might not ever return home."

The small black cat shivered. His tone of voice was insinuating, evil. It made her fur feel as if something had brushed it the wrong way. She drew a breath and deliberately began washing her paw again to give herself time to think. *I am sure my foster sister and brother knew of the terrible dangers we would all face as we traveled. Ptolemy did not try to hide anything from us. We felt we were indeed chosen by a greater power than we to make this journey.*

"Isn't it peculiar the old cat, that devout religious scholar, did not come with you? Did he know the odds of three unsophisticated cats—such young, naive ones—succeeding, especially without a wiser head to guide you? I would assume his paws would be first upon the path; that is, if he believed his own words about the prophecies."

She narrowed her eyes. "Ptolemy could not accompany us because he has to care for the old astronomer. He would gladly have come with us otherwise."

Asmodeus draped his ugly, broken tail over his forepaw as if it were a toga. He looked at it instead of at Abishag, continuing, "Such loyalty is touching. It warms my heart to hear you speak so highly of the old cat. He will be gratified when I speak to him of your steadfastness."

Abishag snorted. "Ptolemy won't listen to anything you have to say. Now leave before I pounce on you."

With a smile that merely stretched the corners of his mouth, Asmodeus edged close to the cat and leaned toward her ear. "He *will* hear what I have to say to him if I am the only one who returns." The rat slipped into the shadows under the trees once again.

Rising to her feet, Abishag stretched and yawned, doing her best to appear unconcerned in case the wily rat was still watching. Her tail up and her head high, she calmly walked back to Gracus's quarters. The other two cats would not know of the worries the rat's whispers had caused to reappear, nor how fast her little heart was beating.

8

ANOTHER TWO WEEKS passed. Gracus purchased Polla and then moved them all into larger quarters, stolidly enduring the good-natured ribbing of his men.

They had been at the garrison headquarters now for seven weeks. Ira's leg was healed and strong once again even though the long bone was crooked.

"As long as it doesn't keep me from marching with the men, I don't care," he told his foster sisters. Kezia rolled her eyes.

"I don't think anyone would mistake you for a Roman soldier, Ira," she told him, cuffing him lightly with her paw. She settled herself in their basket again and yawned.

Gracus suddenly appeared in the doorway. Polla looked up from laboriously stitching a *tunica* for him and smiled.

"You have received your new orders, master," she stated, judging circumstances from the look upon his face.

"I have, and we go to the harbor in two days, to sail for Tyre. From there I shall proceed to Zeugma, to assist in training men for the legions in Anatolia. That may assist my career exceedingly, for those eight legions are responsible for guarding the trade routes to the far lands and protecting our eastern borders."

"What is this Tyre?" Polla asked. "And what do you mean, that you shall train the men? You do not go alone, forgetting us!"

"Your command of the language is surely increasing."

Gracus grinned at her. "Most especially if you now can argue in Latin instead of your mother tongue."

The three cats sat up abruptly from dozing in their basket. A chilly breeze that morning had sent them indoors instead of outside under the trees as usual.

"What is he talking about?" Kezia whispered.

"Shhh!" Ira hissed. "I want to hear our new orders!"

"*His* new orders," Abishag corrected the other black cat. "Remember, we're supposed to be with him only to find the Messiah."

Gracus was explaining to Polla their upcoming travels.

"Tyre is the biggest port in all of the Roman Empire. You will see galleons, huge warships, and many other ships and boats. Every soldier going to war or to serve in farther lands must pass through Tyre. And Zeugma! What I hear from other commanders is that my pay will suffice to purchase us a fine house upon the hillside and enjoy some of the best things the gods choose to share with us."

Polla threw her arms about his neck. "You do intend to take us with you! You do not mean to forget us and depart us here!"

Gracus laughed. "My favored one, your mastery of Latin deserts you when you grow excited. I will not leave you nor forget you, for I cannot leave behind my heart."

Kezia sighed. "He loves her! Isn't that wonderful? Now we have a real home, with two people to love us and a servant to look after us."

Abishag shook her head. "We travel with them only to find the Christ child. Yes, they have been very good to us. But we must fulfill the prophecy."

Kezia yawned. "Oh, quit worrying so about the prophecies. You're beginning to sound like Ptolemy."

"I wish he were with us," Abishag murmured, watching Citus as the servant moved about the room, already beginning to sort things for the trip. *Finally, we have a way to the harbor and passage. And I will not believe the awful things Asmodeus whispered about Ptolemy. He would not have sent us on this journey if he did not believe we would return to him.*

The next day Gracus went alone to the harbor, to arrange passage for three humans, his chariot and horse, and the cats, for neither he nor Polla wished to leave them behind.

Striding along amid the ships being loaded and unloaded, bundles and amphorae cradled in nets pulled up by men sweating in the humid air of the harbor, Gracus hoped to find a good ship with an honest captain. Shouts and curses in strange languages sounded in his ears, and odd creatures shrieked from cages sitting on the docks; once, something pursued by a seaman scuttled past his feet in their leather *caligae* as he continued his search.

So far the ships and captains he recognized he did not wish to sail with; as a veteran soldier in the service of the emperor, he had some experience already with travel upon the Mediterranean Sea.

Suddenly a heavy hand that lacked half of three fingers fell upon his shoulder, and he turned abruptly to face whoever had accosted him.

"Seeking passage, are you?" the man demanded, craning his neck closer to Gracus so that the man's one functioning eye could see him clearly. A hideous scar that ran the length of his face brought attention to his milk-white left eye. His scowl revealed a front tooth banded in gold, and he kept his hand upon Gracus's shoulder.

"Alexos!" Gracus exclaimed and pulled the captain's remnant of a hand from his shoulder into a warm handshake with both his own. "I am blessed by the gods yet again, for I would dare sail with you in pursuit of Poseidon's treasure, should you desire that golden hoard!"

The captain abruptly dropped the handshake and spat into the dirty waters of the harbor. "Take no offense, great Poseidon," he said to counter Gracus's compliment to his skill in sailing. "This land dweller knows nothing of the powers of your seas. Do not vent your anger at his ignorance upon myself and my poor ship."

The two men took their midday meal together in a tavern, and Gracus regaled his friend with tales of life in the barracks with his oddly assorted family.

"So you wish to bring your cats along with us," Alexos remarked as Gracus finished his cup of wine.

"Is there something amiss?"

The Greek sea captain grinned, making his face even more hideous to look upon. "Not at all. In fact, I shall be pleased to have your cats aboard, for this time I sail with a full shipload of grain."

Gracus raised his eyebrows. "And you do not wish to sail with a shipload of mice and rats."

Alexos nodded. "Your cats will be more welcome, actually, than yourselves. For I shall not have to feed them." He laughed.

The men parted and Gracus hurried back to his quarters, well pleased with finding not just a very capable captain with whom to sail, but a friend of many years.

Early the next morning Gracus flicked the reins across the back of his horse, and his chariot caught the first rays of the rising sun.

Behind the chariot came another horse pulling a small cart with Citus, Polla, and the three cats in their basket.

"So that's what we looked like as we entered the outlying parts of Lepcis Magna," Kezia commented, admiring the gleaming chariot, polished and bearing Gracus as befitted a warrior. "I wish all of the city could have seen us in our grandeur!"

Abishag settled herself to sleep in the basket while

Kezia and Ira stood with their front paws upon the basket rim, looking at the sights. *At least we are now started on our way again. I hope we are still following the prophecies correctly. It has been so long since Ptolemy first taught me, I fear forgetting some of his directions.*

Gracus's few possessions and the fewer yet of his servant and slave filled only part of the cart bed. In the darkest corner of the cart Asmodeus crouched beneath a wineskin. *Finally, a taste of adventure once again. A few other rats should be on board, and they may have many amusing tales with which to regale me. And if the seafaring life suits me, I will abandon my post of nursemaid to these country simpletons and remain aboard. Ah, the exotic foods I may yet sample!*

Aboard the *Oceanos*, Gracus and Polla were given a cabin next to Alexos's captain's quarters. Citus would bunk with the seamen, either above or belowdecks depending upon the weather. The weather itself would determine whether their passage was easy or difficult, as well as the duration of their voyage.

Several of the sailors muttered among themselves when they first spied Citus carrying the basket of cats aboard. Alexos, who saw more with his one good eye than most captains who still had both, noticed this. *Unrest among my sailors? Ah, again those two I but recently signed. Well, I shall not be sorry if they find another ship once we reach Tyre, for I am heartily tired of their whispers and moans. I will deal with this on the morrow.*

At dawn the next day the ship was fully loaded with her cargo of grain and passengers. Alexos poured wine for all aboard and then carefully poured the first cup into the harbor water, asking Poseidon for a safe journey and fair weather. He next lifted his own wine cup and poured a few drops onto the plate Citus used to feed the cats.

"And your blessing, O mighty Poseidon, on these your servants also, for they will rid my ship of vermin, and I shall bring rich gifts to your temple in Tyre." Sailors stared as Ira sauntered up to the plate and stuck his tongue into the wine drops.

"You must take a sip, too," he hissed at his foster sisters. "Otherwise, we will offend their gods and the sailors will fear punishment for the entire ship." Abishag and Kezia immediately lapped up the remaining drops.

Alexos pointed to the three grouped around their plate.

"You see? These are not ordinary wharf cats or household lap cats. They will bring us luck on this voyage, as they have already brought luck to Gracus in his new orders, which will advance his career." He told his men of Gracus's dream about two black cats and one tabby, waiting for him beside the road to Lepcis Magna. He spoke of Ira's broken leg and Kezia's near-drowning, concluding both his speech and the ceremony by saying, "Do not harm them; it is obvious they are under the gods' protection."

Citus stood listening to the captain and thinking of how large the ship's rats were; he had seen a few as he stabled the chariot horse belowdecks. He'd brought strong, well-tanned leather with which to make a new harness for Gracus's horse during the four- to six-week journey. *I will have plenty of leather to spare. The male cat needs a leather harness to protect his chest and neck, since his crooked leg slows his pounce a bit, and I can easily fashion wide collars for the two females. They will have some protection from rat bites in that manner.*

"I still say two black cats mean two demons are now aboard," one seaman whispered to his friend as the command to sail was passed. "What real cats would drink wine?"

"But a tabby is reputed to bring good luck," his friend replied.

"So we throw the two demons overboard and keep the tabby. No harm in that, is there?" And the first sailor nodded to the other as he went to his station, preparing to hoist anchor.

Just before dawn the next day, sailors on watch were surprised by a small parade of triumphant cats, each carrying a dead rat nearly as large as themselves. They laid the carcasses in front of Alexos's door and then scratched on the door of the next cabin. Polla opened it, and the cats went inside Gracus's quarters to lick their wounds and sleep.

When Alexos discovered the dead vermin, he insisted Citus take a fresh-caught fish to the cats as their reward. Then the captain skinned the rats, tied their tails together, and hung the hides from a rope flung overboard.

Asmodeus ground his remaining teeth in rage. "How dare he preserve the skins of our comrades!" he shouted to the seafaring rats that night, deep in the hold of the ship. "This is outrage! This is deliberate affront!"

"What's he screamin' about?" One rat nudged another just as they prepared to gnaw their way into a tasty bundle of tallow candles.

"Don't know. Can't care," answered his fellow rat, and then he swore as he saw Ira slip into the hold. "Hades! We're in for it now—run!"

Three more rat carcasses and two dead mice were in front of Alexos's door the next morning. Kezia lingered for a few minutes. *Those two mice are so plump,* she thought longingly. *The fish yesterday was delicious, but not nearly enough for all three of us. It isn't as if Alexos is going to eat them. Surely he wouldn't mind if I had only one.*

Just then the captain opened his door. With a pleased exclamation, he bent to look at the night's catch and spied Kezia. He held out a hand to her.

"Ah, pretty one. You and your companions have hunted successfully again! I thank you, for the merchant receiving the grain promised me a reward if his goods were delivered without rat droppings."

Kezia wrinkled her nose at the thought but wound

herself around Alexos's ankles and purred. *I may be a lady cat, but I do know how to kill vermin,* she told him silently.

"You act as if you understood my words," he said, surprised, and gently patted her. "You may have the mice for breakfast, if you wish," he added. "I save the rats' hides because there is a peculiar merchant in Tyre who buys them for use in medicine."

Kezia pounced on the mice and ate them quickly, looking up at Alexos as she finished. "You are sent by the gods," he murmured. "I will see that today's fish sent to you is a larger one than yesterday. Hunting is hard work."

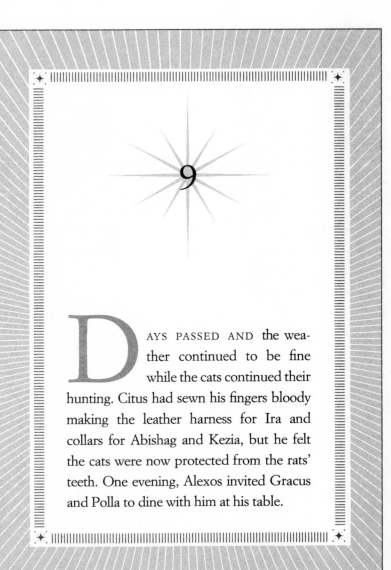

9

DAYS PASSED AND the weather continued to be fine while the cats continued their hunting. Citus had sewn his fingers bloody making the leather harness for Ira and collars for Abishag and Kezia, but he felt the cats were now protected from the rats' teeth. One evening, Alexos invited Gracus and Polla to dine with him at his table.

"I am pleased with your cats, Gracus," he began, after they had enjoyed fresh-caught fish with sauce and other delicacies, for Alexos believed in feeding himself and his passengers and crew well. "Would you consider parting with the tabby, thus allowing her to continue to serve aboard my ship?"

Gracus frowned. "If I could be sure it would not offend the gods, you would have your cat within my next breath, old friend," he said. "But I do not know what they wish. Have you someone aboard skilled in reading entrails?"

Now Alexos frowned. "No, regrettably, I do not." He thought for a moment. "But I am sure I may find someone in Tyre. We shall go together to ask."

"Agreed."

The humans hadn't seen the tabby crouched by the open door to Alexos's quarters. Kezia's small head drooped, as did her thoughts. *No one has asked me about this. Spend the rest of my life on this smelly ship? I would have to put up with this ugly collar forever. What if we were caught by pirates—they nearly killed Alexos; just look at his disfigured face and crippled hand. He is a kind man, a good merchant seaman, but he has no servants, no real luxuries; nor*

does he feel the lack of them. Besides,
we—I—promised Ptolemy we would stay
together until we found the Messiah.

The next day saw a sudden squall brew
itself up in the middle of the Mediterranean:
a violent disturbance that nearly forced the
Oceanos down to the sea's depths. The storm was so
fierce, Gracus told Citus to stay with Polla in the cabin
and to fasten a lid upon the cats' basket. "If we have to
abandon ship," he bellowed so as to be heard over the
shrieking winds, "the cats will all be rescued together
that way!" He turned then and fought his way across the
deck to where Alexos stood, hands on the ship's tiller
and feet planted firmly on the deck.

"This eye says it's a bad squall," he greeted Gracus
and tilted his head to the left. "And the one that can see
prophesies no better. I think perhaps you must keep your
cats. Obviously the gods do not want them divided!"
A sudden huge wave washed over the side of the ship
and carried away three seamen. Cries of fear rang out
and bits of hastily mumbled prayers were heard, too,
as sailors clung to ropes or the lowered sails, and the
wildly heaving ship seemed to groan its last with every

lashing of rain. "Get back to your cabin, Gracus! This storm is for seafaring men, not soldiers, brave though they may be."

"What of my horse?" Gracus leaned close to Alexos and shouted to be barely heard above the waves and wind.

"He must fend for himself until we ride this out," Alexos shouted in turn. "I am sorry for the beast, but no one can get belowdecks now—the waves are coming over the sides so rapidly, they could wash into an open hatch and sink the entire ship in seconds."

Gracus suddenly tried to fight his way to the side as it tilted up; but he lost his footing and his breakfast in one precipitous drop of the entire ship, as she crested a wave only to have it fall below her.

Polla sat on the cabin floor when the storm first blew up and tied one end of a strong rope about her waist and the other end to a metal ring in the wall placed there for just such emergencies. Then she took the cats' basket and set it on her lap, wrapping her arms about it. She crooned to the cats and sang softly to them in her native language. Citus copied her and tied himself to another ring on the opposite wall. He marveled at her composure, and finally his curiosity overcame him.

"How is it that you stay so calm in the midst of this? We may all be dashed to pieces at any moment!"

She turned her head and the thick blond braid swung across her shoulder. "This is a storm much like the one that beset the slave ship I was brought in, as we were close to the other shore of the sea," she told him.

"So you have survived a storm such as this before!"

"No, I have survived a shipwreck before," she corrected him. "There were only myself, the captain, and five other men who clung to the main mast until another ship found us. Two of the men died when they were pulled aboard because their injuries were too terrible."

Citus covered his eyes with his hands for a minute. "May the gods in their mercy spare you once more, Polla." Just then the door burst open and Gracus staggered through it. He took the cats' basket out of Polla's arms and struggled back on deck once more.

Standing beside Alexos, who still battled with the tiller to keep the ship from keeling over, Gracus tore off the cover of the basket. He held the basket to the skies and shouted, "See, O gods and goddesses! Those whom you have favored for so long are indeed aboard this small ship! Grant them safe passage, I beg you!"

The wind dropped abruptly. Gracus looked into the skies as the rain began pelting down, and he laughed. Alexos pried his numbed hands free from the ship's tiller and leaned against the rail, joining Gracus in relieved laughter. "Rain we can deal with," Alexos gasped, the water pouring down his face and running into his mouth. "The furred ones are truly in the gods' favor!" The cats began yowling, indignant at growing wetter by the second, and then scrambled out of the basket as Gracus set it on the deck. They dashed for the cabin as Polla pulled the heavy door open, and ran past her feet to the much drier interior.

"That rain was cold," Kezia fussed, trying to lick her wet fur dry. Shivering, Abishag agreed, while Ira shook himself repeatedly. Citus untied and coiled the ropes he and Polla had used to secure themselves, and then took the blanket in which he slept out on the deck at night.

"Here, little ones," he said to the unhappy cats. "Use your rough tongues to dry yourselves and then I shall bundle you into this blanket, for I also think you may have saved our lives by being favored of the gods." He wrapped them well in the heavy wool, and they soon dozed off. *There, you see,* Kezia thought as she fell asleep. *Alexos, poor human, did not even think to warm us again. How could I manage without Citus?*

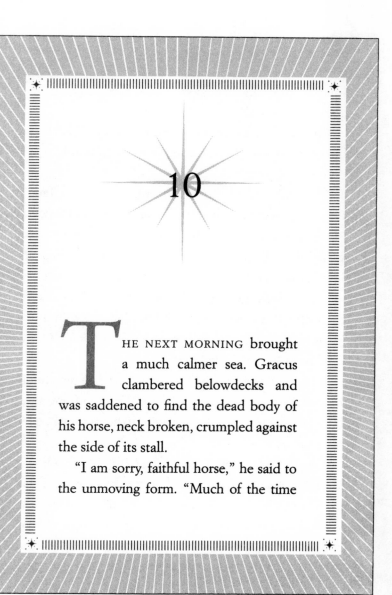

10

THE NEXT MORNING brought a much calmer sea. Gracus clambered belowdecks and was saddened to find the dead body of his horse, neck broken, crumpled against the side of its stall.

"I am sorry, faithful horse," he said to the unmoving form. "Much of the time you were very brave, a good chariot horse. Perhaps the gods needed you."

Citus appeared beside the centurion. "We must bury him at sea; else the cook may try to boil him for dinner."

"No, he was too good an animal for that fate," Gracus agreed. He called to several seamen above deck. "I will pay you for your help, to have my horse buried with Poseidon and Neptune instead of suffering an ignominious end in the stew pot."

Ira watched the carcass being slung over the side of the ship. "It is surprising he did not kill me, with those great feet of his," he said to himself. "Ptolemy's One God must have shielded me."

Asmodeus interrupted Ira's musings while remaining hidden in a coiled rope on deck. "No, you are alive because you are too great a warrior to be vanquished by an ordinary enemy."

"But he wasn't my enemy," Ira said. "After all, *you* were the one who frightened him into rearing. And you *are* my enemy!" He pounced on the pile of rope, but Asmodeus evaded him and ran for the opposite side of the ship. He dived down a rat hole and waited for the black cat to begin a vigil at the entrance. "You have to come out sometime," Ira told the invisible rat and settled himself to wait.

Asmodeus smirked to himself. He enjoyed placing doubts and fears into their minds, causing the cats to worry.

"What an honor—to be pounced upon and devoured by the greatest warrior this poor ship has yet seen!" he began.

Ira sighed. "Don't try compliments, Asmodeus. They won't change my mind about catching you."

"No, no, no—what I tell you are not mere compliments, but facts. You are in truth a great warrior; you marched and learned with the other soldiers strategy and planning—or perhaps not. Even with Ptolemy, you never did pay close attention to your lessons, did you?"

"I did, too!" Ira protested. "It's just that I had other important things to do. So of course the girls listened to Ptolemy more. I had to learn to pounce and to kill far more readily than the two females. They lack my instinct for the death blow," he concluded, a bit smugly.

"And you do indeed possess that, my young cat," Asmodeus agreed, his voice silken. "Thanks to you, I no longer have any companions with whom to pass a quiet hour or even to share a bit of bread—"

"A bit of bread!" Ira laughed. "You and your disgusting companions were destroying several bushels of grain a day, with your droppings fouling what you did not stuff into your greedy faces."

"Well, they are all gone now," Asmodeus snarled. He drew a deep breath, trying to calm himself. "I alone and a few frightened or injured mice are all that remain."

"So what do you want?"

"A truce?"

"Why should I grant you a truce?"

"Because when we arrive in Tyre, I shall leave the ship and live ashore the rest of my days," Asmodeus promised.

"You aren't going to return to our tower outside of Lepcis Magna?"

"No, and neither are you."

"What do you mean?" Ira asked, startled.

"You cannot convince me that a warrior of your

stature, of your hunting skills, would meekly consent to live out the rest of his days in a dreary tower, where nothing exciting ever happens. Unless you count the odd butterfly or beetle that sometimes becomes bewildered and lost within its walls? Or perhaps," the rat added nastily, "you want to listen to Ptolemy maunder on and on about prophecies and religions and parchment scrolls until he draws his last breath. You will be too aged yourself by then to set forth once more to see the world."

Unwillingly, Ira thought back to the weeks and weeks of lessons he'd endured, listening to Ptolemy's patient instructions. *Those weeks were boring. I'm glad Abishag listened so carefully; sometimes I got to doze in the sun instead of having to pay attention every second.*

He shifted his position beside the rat hole. "A soldier must do what is right," he replied.

"Is it right for the old cat to expect you to give up everything you have fought for during this long journey and submit to his learned knowledge once you return? You cannot convince me that you do not long to stay with Gracus, because you and he are of the same mind," Asmodeus said craftily. "Two warriors, marching off to foreign lands and tremendous battles. Think of it! Think of the cheers that would greet you as you returned triumphant from your latest campaign, standing regally in Gracus's chariot and being admired by the crowd."

The picture the clever rat painted became very clear to Ira's imagination. He envisioned himself and Gracus attired in new armor. The fact that he could not have borne the weight of the metal armor, even had it been made so tiny, never occurred to him. He basked in the imaginary adulation and reveled in his status as an acclaimed warrior. Bowls of heavy cream and plump doves would be his breakfast daily.

"And you would forgo all of this, for a corner in a musty tower, glad to catch a handful of warmth from a stingy fire in the dead of winter."

Ira shivered, completely caught up in the rat's machinations. *I cannot return to that! I must stay with Gracus—he understands what a soldier needs. I cannot return to the tower. The girls will have to go without me.*

He turned and left the rat hole, thinking deeply as he retraced his steps to Gracus's cabin. He didn't hear Asmodeus snicker as he watched the young cat leave.

Later that same morning, Kezia was having a fruitless search for a mouse. Although she wasn't really hungry, she was bored and wanted something more challenging than her fifth bath of the day. She was down in the hold, searching and sniffing, when she heard Alexos's step upon the ship's ladder. *Well, at least he will talk to me and pet me and tell me how pretty I am,* the little tabby thought and ran out to greet the captain.

He did see her, even in the poor light and with his limited vision. "Good morning, little lady!" he called across the sacks of grain. "I am but counting my stores— as you yourself are, perhaps?" And he chuckled, rightly assuming she was mouse hunting again. He started to move one of the grain sacks when he realized the leather thong at the mouth of it was untied. He climbed up on top of the neighboring stack of grain sacks so he could reach and retie the thong—and suddenly screamed horribly. A snake had stuck its head out of the mouth of the untied sack and was flicking its tongue at Alexos.

"I am a lady cat, but I also know how to kill snakes!" Kezia cried, and it seemed as if she flew to the stack of grain sacks. She caught the snake before it could crawl away, seizing it behind its head and holding it firmly.

The snake thrashed and fought, striking her several times with loops of its hard body. It flailed itself free of the grain sack and kept thrashing.

Alexos, pale and sweating, looked around frantically for any sort of weapon. "I must not let the snake kill her!" He spotted a trident and grabbed it up. He slashed wildly at the snake, not even hearing the running feet of his men in his panic.

Kezia nimbly sidestepped the trident hitting dangerously close to her and kept her hold on the snake. Finally, after being hacked many times by the tines and with Kezia's sharp teeth penetrating its spinal cord, the snake died, and the cat dropped it at Alexos's feet. He turned a ghastly shade of green but managed to stammer out, "Th-thank you, most honored lady! You have saved me from a terrible death!"

Some of Alexos's seamen ran up just then, panting, and the captain began relating the wondrous tale of the cat's courage to his circle of listeners, who looked in awe at the tabby. Kezia purred and sat down to wash herself, for she felt she stank badly of snake. As she washed her right ear, it stung, and when she looked at her paw, it was covered in blood. Just then Alexos turned and saw her paw.

"The snake has bitten her!" he bellowed and rushed to her. Anxiously, he examined Kezia, searching for the marks of fangs. "Praise Poseidon! The snake has not harmed her—but I myself must have hurt her with the trident." He knelt in front of her as she sat on some sacks of grain. "Forgive me, my little one. My witless attempts to help you kill the snake have injured you. My sorrow is deep." Tears stood in his eye as he carefully washed her torn ear with wine and then tied a soft bit of cloth about her head, to hold the ear close so it could heal.

After Alexos's ministrations, Kezia crept away to the cats' basket in Gracus's quarters, where the other two found her after searching for an hour.

"Now *you* are acclaimed a warrior," Ira said, dashing up to the basket and speaking half enviously and half in jest.

"Are you still hurting?" Abishag asked. "Can we help by licking it for you?"

Kezia showed her two closest friends a woebegone face.

"I am now hideous," she said to them and whimpered. "My appearance is no longer comely, and I am ashamed. I was a beautiful kitten, a lovely youngster, and a graceful lady cat. Now I am as ugly—as ugly as poor Alexos."

"You need never be ashamed of your looks when you have saved a friend's life," Ira said stoutly. But secretly he wondered whether his foster sister was being punished for her immense vanity.

"What have they tied about your head?" Abishag asked.

"Alexos said it would make my ear heal faster, but I do not think so. It hurts and burns, Abishag. Please do something!" Kezia cried.

The patient Abishag finally worked the bandage off Kezia's head, then she licked her torn ear until Kezia fell asleep.

"Will she be all right?" Ira asked Abishag as they left Gracus's cabin to go claim their usual fish for dinner.

"I think she will be just fine," Abishag said. "And if the cut becomes infected, Polla will tend to her ear, for she loves Kezia, too." *I wish someone cared for me as Alexos does Kezia,* Abishag thought sadly. *He was trying to defend her from the snake, rather than killing the serpent because of the threat to himself. And Gracus and Polla dearly love Ira, their "little soldier." I wish someone loved me. I miss Ptolemy, and even the old astronomer. I wish our journey was over. I want to go home . . .*

That night Gracus had another dream of the cats. He had gone to his bunk in the cabin thinking about Alexos and the snake. *He is astonishingly afraid of serpents,* Gracus thought. *I wonder what has happened in the past to make him fear them so.* In his dream, he saw past events repeated: Ira, hurt and lying in the dusty road; Kezia, half drowned when Citus rescued her after Abishag had clung valiantly to her to prevent the tabby from being swept away in the current; and now Kezia again, rescuing Alexos from sure death by snakebite. Then it seemed he entered a path or a corridor— he saw the three cats walking away from him. When he called them, they ran from him, not stopping to look at him or even turning their heads. A long, long time passed in his dream, and yet he still searched, looking at each small black cat when he saw another one, searching for Ira with his crooked leg. He woke after a restless night and lay there sweating. *The gods obviously want them to stay together. But then why would I search for only the one? My heart knows that I am fondest of my "little soldier," true, but I would not separate the three from one another.*

11

TYRE AT LAST! The seamen cheered as their ship sailed into the mouth of the harbor, and each man insisted on touching all three cats before disembarking. The two seamen who had muttered about having the cats aboard presented the felines with a wooden cage, whittled from a small cask, filled with crickets as a delicacy for them.

"Where to now, Alexos?" Gracus asked the captain as they stood for a moment on the deck.

"Well, I am not—by the gods! That ship! Look, Gracus! It is a ship of my countrymen—it is from Athens. But who sails upon it?"

A great, graceful ship was highlighted by the rays of the morning sun.

"It must indeed be Kaspar!" cried Alexos. "Come, Gracus—come with me and meet a man unlike any other you have met."

Gracus shrugged. "Well, why not? I assume you will be in harbor for a day or so, at least until you have met with your grain merchant and settled accounts. May we all stay aboard with you until I report to my new commander?"

"Yes, of course you shall stay with me aboard ship! Remember, I was to ask a reader of entrails or an oracle if your little tabby, who saved my life, might be safely parted from her companions and remain with me." Alexos paused for a moment. "In truth, we received our answer when the storm quieted upon the three's appearance. But I shall send word to Kaspar, who is also my kinsman, and ask him to dine with us this evening.

You shall be amazed at the stories he has to tell us. He is revered as a wise man in my native land."

Gracus nodded. "I must speak to this man also. I have had yet another dream about the cats and confess I am puzzled as to its meaning."

"Then be certain to relate it to Kaspar this night. He will divine what it foretells."

That night everyone dined very well, as Alexos had hired three cooks from neighboring vessels to produce a feast "fit for a king," as he told them, and sent men to the markets for supplies. Kezia, Abishag, and Ira were clustered close together in their basket, trying not to fall asleep after their own miniature feast.

Over cups of fragrant hot wine laced with spices, Gracus told Kaspar of his first and then his latest dream about the cats, all of whom woke abruptly when they realized he was speaking of them. Ira began to scramble out of the basket.

He reached Gracus's caligae just as the centurion said quietly, "If it would not offend the gods, I would be greatly tempted to keep my 'little soldier,' as I call him. See, he comes to me to be petted"—here he leaned down and gently caressed Ira's sleek sides—"and seems to respond to my very thoughts about him. It is almost as if he speaks Latin."

Kaspar nodded. "You have had the protective harness he wears made for him."

"My servant, Citus, crafted it for him, and he wears it as proudly as any plume or badge of honor."

"There are two more, you said?"

"Come, cats!" Gracus called, and Kezia and Abishag jumped out of the basket and ran to Gracus. They all sat at the centurion's feet to watch faces and listen.

"I do not wish to alarm you," Kaspar began, speaking slowly, "but somehow these are cats about which many dreams are being cast."

Alexos turned to face his kinsman with his good eye. "What do you mean?"

"For months now, I have watched the heavens. There are signs and portents of great events about to occur; a magnificent star is in the east and nightly grows brighter."

Abishag caught her breath. *The star! The star Ptolemy spoke of—he was right! I thought it was getting bigger!*

"I await two companions: Melchior from Alexandria and Balthazar from Antioch. They are to meet me here in the harbor and then we shall purchase camels and set off on the last leg of our journey."

Alexos waved a hired servant over to fill the wine cups again. "Where are you going? And why have you said there is something significant concerning these three cats?"

"As for the cats specifically, I know not. I only know that I have dreamed of them accompanying us as we travel to find the Messiah."

In the stunned silence that followed his words, the cats' eyes were as wide and round as any ocean pearls.

Abishag nearly wept. "We are to go with them," she whispered to Kezia and Ira. "Did you hear? We shall be taken with them as they search for the King of Kings. Just as Ptolemy said."

Gracus swallowed hard. "The Messiah?"

"Yes, He is soon to be born Who shall rule the world."

The centurion could not grasp the staggering implications all at once. "He is then the next emperor?"

"I do not think He will necessarily rule upon this earth. But I do know that myself and my companions have been chosen by the One God to complete this journey and then tell others of what we have learned. Look."

Kaspar held out his left hand to Gracus and Polla. Alexos retreated to the shadows as the other two gazed at Kaspar's strong, open hand. Upon the lined palm a star was emblazoned clearly.

"Melchior and Balthazar also have this mark upon their palms. None of us would have known about this common star were it not for my kinsman here—come, do not try to fold yourself within the darkness, Alexos!"

Alexos leaned across the table, his face within the glow of candlelight once again. "It but serves to show how a garrulous seaman can spread tales, my Kaspar."

Kaspar laughed. "He has denied any part of being an agent to speed the old prophecies to fruition. But to return to other signs: Melchior brings three doves, which were sent to him in the middle of an unusually violent storm in Alexandria, and about which he had dreamed the night beforehand. Balthazar brings three rings—one of wood, one of stone, and one of metal— which he directed a servant to dig up from the roots of an old cedar tree after having dreamed of the treasure beneath it."

Ira felt the skin along his backbone ripple in a shiver. *This is almost scaring me,* he thought. *Surely the old cat at home couldn't have known of all of this. Or if he did, he would have told Abishag, for she was the one, of all of us, Ptolemy loved most. I wonder if she's ever realized that.*

The tabby cat was lost in daydreams of splendor. *This man, this wise man, as the humans have called him, also says we go to discover the King of Kings. I am going to live in a palace after all! I shall have silk pillows to sleep upon and jeweled collars by the dozen.*

"And my dream was very simple: I saw three cats— two black and one tabby—traveling with us, in search of the place where the star will come to rest."

Soon the dinner participants separated. Kaspar promised he would return for the cats as soon as his other companions were ready to set forth. "I shall have baskets crafted for them, so they may ride upon camels and move swiftly through the desert night."

Gracus chuckled at the thought. "You must see that the little soldier's basket has lower sides, then. For he does want to see where he is going; I think he plans his campaign ahead of need. And he marched many miles with my men as I trained them. He may wish to walk at times."

Asmodeus, crouched in the thickest shadows, spat and curled his lip. *"He may wish to walk at times." My stomach heaves at the simper! Curse them! I must plan carefully so I may also ride and not walk. I would dwell most happily in only one of those palaces that continually are promised to these undeserving, juvenile upstarts. Prophecies! Bah!*

Once back in their cabin, Gracus soon fell fast asleep. Moving quietly so as not to disturb him, Polla sat on the floor and held Ira and Kezia in her lap while Abishag leaned against her knee. "Miss you I shall, most painfully," she told them softly. "Were I not but an ignorant slave, I could add my own predictions for you, as I know them in my heart. I dare not speak them aloud, lest I give you hopes or fears of a future that may not come to pass. At least you will see wonders."

She turned to Abishag and spoke into her ear. "You will return to love someday. Keep my words and let them guide you when you despair." She placed her hands upon her abdomen and smiled at the black cat. "My home country says women who grow heavy with child see things other women do not. I will have a child in seven months, and in my thoughts, I have seen five fat kittens tumbling and playing about your paws. Their fur is strangely marked, but they will bring you great joy."

LESS THAN A week later, Alexos's ship had been emptied of its golden grain and the promised bonus paid. He was pleased with life in general and joked with Gracus as the centurion walked restlessly about the deck.

"You must get a legion of your own soon, my friend, else you will surely wear my ship's boards thin with your pacing."

Gracus snorted. "No legion command for me at any near time, Alexos. But I would hear the order for me to report for duty. Inaction tires me more than battle."

The two men turned at sudden noises from the dockside crowd and saw Kaspar and four servants coming toward the ship. When he waved, the three cats leaped from where they had been lounging in the shadows and ran down the ship's plank. No one saw Asmodeus silently slip down a mooring rope and scurry into a heavy bundle one of Kaspar's servants had set down for a moment.

Gracus watched them as they hurried to meet Kaspar.

"I swear to you, Alexos, they heard and comprehended our entire conversation of a few nights ago." Then a lump rose in Gracus's throat, for, contrary to his dream, Ira looked back at the centurion. The black cat held the man's gaze for a long minute, then raised his crooked left leg and tilted his paw. The Roman returned the salute, and Ira turned and trotted after Kaspar, the servants, and the other two cats.

12

THE CARAVAN SET out upon the trip to Jerusalem two days after the cats had left Alexos's ship. Kaspar kept Ira close beside him on his camel, in a low-sided basket as Gracus had advised, while Kezia had her own basket upon Melchior's camel and Abishag was with Balthazar.

It felt odd to the cats to be traveling separately, since they had been journeying as a threesome now for many months. But they met one another at mealtimes and then when the caravan stopped for the evening, and with that they had to be content. Each of the three cats, indeed, had so many of his or her own thoughts to mull over that they really had little time to grow lonely for their accustomed companionship.

The weather grew colder also, and each was glad to curl up in a basket out of the piercing wind, as the wise men followed the brightest star in the eastern sky.

Two weeks into the journey all the travelers sat about a welcome fire, blazing in the darkness that was the desert after sundown.

The men had their evening meal and then listened as one of their servants began a plaintive tune upon a small fife.

"Have you brought a gift for the Messiah, Kaspar?" Balthazar asked as the last notes faded.

Kaspar nodded. "From what Melchior has said, we have among us brought gold, frankincense, and myrrh. What will you do with the three doves?"

Melchior raised his head and looked into the night

sky before answering. "I know not. I had a beautiful cage fashioned for them, of gold wire and tiny jewels. Yet somehow they seem not appropriate for a babe, unless they represent the peace He is to bring our sad, war-torn earth."

"I confess I myself am puzzled as to the significance of the three rings I dreamed of and then brought along, in answer to my heart's urging," Balthazar commented.

"The rings do represent three elements," Kaspar replied.

"Yes, but what need would a Messiah have for ordinary articles such as they? For they have no jewels nor value to them that I may perceive. The metal one is but a harder ring than the one of wood, yet still more malleable than the one of stone." Balthazar's very voice sounded perplexed.

Kaspar nodded at the cats, who were dozing in the warmth of the fire. "Well, if it is apparent need or use you are seeking, what of them? We have responded to dreams as we felt we were bidden by the old prophecies and by the One God. And we are following that beautiful star as we were also bidden. Surely when we reach our journey's end we shall have all revealed to us!"

With that hope voiced aloud, the human and feline members of the camp soon settled to sleep. Kaspar had thoughtfully brought along the big basket Gracus had originally provided them, and the three cats slept warmly each night within the folds of the rough wool cloak.

Before dawn, however, Abishag woke and, resting her chin on the edge of the basket, watched the glorious star in the east. *It seems to be traveling just ahead of us now,* she thought, half asleep still. *It is as if we are beckoned onward by it, to find the King of Kings and to present Him with our gifts . . . To think I am actually on the last leg of such a profound journey. We have had such generous help from all the humans now in our lives. I know Ira suffered with his poor broken leg, and Kezia's ear was painful until it healed. Now it is crumpled and she isn't as pretty as she was—but we are all alive and well, considering. I want to hurry and find the Messiah—and then hurry even faster to return home and tell Ptolemy all we have seen and done and heard. I hope he is well, too. And that he watches the same star, at least what he can see of it from so far away. Does he wonder about us and how we are doing? Does he—does he miss me? I miss him very much.*

A light breakfast and they were off once again, the strong camels traveling many more miles in a day than man or cat could have done on foot. That day seemed a longer one than most; the men shifted in their saddles and the cats were restless in their baskets as the hours wore on. Finally, at a tiny oasis, the call came to dismount and make camp for the night. Riders waited for the camels to lower themselves to the sandy soil; with much groaning and snorting, the great beasts settled themselves and their burdens on the ground.

Ira hopped out of his basket as soon as he judged his crooked leg could bear the shock of his landing. After he stretched, he flung himself onto the bank of a sandy wash that wound through the oasis. On his back, he wriggled until he was covered with silt, thus completing a most satisfying back scratch despite his harness. Rolling to his feet, he went looking for Kezia and Abishag.

Kezia began sneezing when Ira bounded up to her, shaking small puffs of silt from his fur as he jumped.

"Ira! You are as dirty as three human boys could be!" She sneezed again. "Please go shake off the dirt—somewhere else."

Ira laughed and twitched his ears rapidly. "I can make dust signals with my ears," he bragged. "Who needs smoke?" The unseen paw that cuffed an ear belonged to Abishag, and Ira whirled, then pulled himself into a menacing crouch. "Watch out, foster sister! I'm in a fierce mood this evening."

Abishag laughed in turn. "You look as if you have brown fur instead of black. No Roman soldier would ever get that dirty."

"No Roman soldier would ever *stay* this dirty," Ira corrected her and shook himself thoroughly. Then he settled down next to one of the pack camels to bathe, while the girls went hunting. Suddenly his upper lip flehmened and he swore—softly, so his sisters wouldn't overhear him.

"By Mars's shield; Asmodeus, how is it you travel so many miles to plague us and yet never lose your stink?"

"Ah, my young soldier cat. You bear your grudges as you would bear your arms—if you could do so." Asmodeus smirked at Ira from behind the bundles of provisions. "And how fare you and your delightful foster sisters?"

"We're fine."

"Good. I am delighted for you. Now that you are a warrior and a world traveler, you should be doing very well indeed. Are you dining as pleasantly as you did aboard Alexos's ship?"

"We don't have fresh fish any longer, silly. This is the desert," Ira answered, resuming his bath.

"But there is plump, fresh dove for the taking."

Ira glared at Asmodeus. "You're disgusting. Those doves are sacred; they are gifts to the Messiah."

"Indeed? So they are not tender, succulent meat, kept for you, a seasoned warrior, in a cage with but a tiny clasp? Are they not fed daily with ripe grain, so they grow plumper yet?"

The black cat's mouth watered in spite of himself. "They are not to be eaten. They are gifts. And don't you bother them either."

"Three gifts for three cats. Imagine how your sisters would praise you for presenting them each with a juicy, tender young bird. They wouldn't have to hunt for themselves, as they're in the process of doing at this very minute. Do they not pity you, since they share their kills with you? You must admit you cannot pounce as well as you could previously."

Ira clenched his teeth as he began to get angry. Then his stomach rumbled, and the rat heard it.

"Last night's dinner, if memory serves me correctly, was but a few locusts; the servants did not think to feed you. Not much for a warrior's rations."

"The legion marches on hard bread and water," Ira said firmly. "I am entitled to that, too. But I do not draw provisions or pay from the quartermaster. I secure my own rations." And without warning, he leaped at the rat, who barely scuttled to safety under another pile of packs.

"You deceitful ingrate!" Asmodeus snarled. "I endeavor to present you with an easily procured dinner, and in turn you try to dine upon me. You've ruined my tail—I won't forget this!"

"I wouldn't eat you if I were starving," Ira said and spat out the tip of Asmodeus's bedraggled tail. "Remember when I caught you before, I told Ptolemy you smelled too bad to eat."

Only curses answered Ira as he strolled away, joining his sisters for their evening hunt. They caught a few beetles but fared very well anyway, as the servants killed and roasted two fat sheep from the flock brought with them upon the journey. Flavored with rich spices and very tender, the meat filled everyone's stomachs nearly to bursting.

Abishag looked at the beautiful star for a long time after everyone else, including the humans, had settled for the night. She started to climb into the basket, which was turned on its side toward the fire, nudging Kezia and Ira over to make a little more room when she paused.

What was that peculiar sound?

She left the basket and listened. The entire camp appeared to be sound asleep; the fire had burned down to a handful of glowing coals. Even the sentries were seated instead of standing. *That's not right. Ira said there must always be someone keeping watch, especially at night.*

The sound came again: a horrible, moaning noise that quickly escalated into a high-pitched quaver of notes that frightened Abishag. And the noise was closer; closer now than when she had first heard it.

She woke Ira and then Kezia. "Something is wrong. There is some strange creature out there—"

An answering call from the other side of the camp served to shake the sleep from Ira's eyes and he bounded out of the basket. "What is that terrible noise?"

The sheep began moving about anxiously and the lead camels raised their heads and snorted softly.

"We must wake the humans," Abishag said practically. "And do so now!" She ran to where Balthazar was sleeping peacefully and began patting his face with a paw. Kezia began licking and nibbling Melchior's fingers.

Ira hurried to Kaspar and butted the wise man's shoulder with his small head. He repeated this until he roused him from a deep sleep. "What is wrong, little

soldier?" he asked sleepily— and then sat straight up as the eerie cry sounded across the sands and the oasis once again.

"Wolves!" he gasped and leaped to his feet, throwing his blankets aside. "Wolves!" he shouted, and the entire camp woke, just as the sheep bleated in terror and crowded against an outcropping of rock. A huge wolf brazenly snatched the smallest sheep of the flock and dragged it away from the oasis; it kicked and struggled briefly until the wolf's hold on its throat deprived it of life. The sentries snatched up their spears and cudgels and began patrolling the outer rim of their small encampment.

Melchior and Balthazar also grasped cudgels and quickly herded the sheep into a small band. Kaspar took a torch and began setting smaller fires in a wide circle about the camp. Servants urged the camels to their feet and brought them close to the fire, which had been rekindled and now blazed mightily. In the darkness, the sounds of fighting, snarling wolves carried through the clear air.

The sheep were brought closest to the fire and then the camels were placed at one side of it. The packs were gathered into a low wall, atop which Ira stationed himself. His foster sisters went to help watch the sheep by the fire.

It grew colder, and the sky began to grow slightly less densely black as the sun started its slow ascent in the east. A light snow had dusted some of the surrounding hills as the travelers slept. Several times Ira saw shadows slipping through those same hills, but the wolves had fallen silent once the camp was awake and on guard.

After the sun rose, the servants prepared breakfast for the camp and half of the hired guards lay down to sleep while the others continued at their posts. Kezia and Abishag went to Ira.

"They caught us sleeping this time in reality," he told them grimly. "I forgot all too soon the lessons Gracus taught me. I will resume standing sentry duty at night."

"What are wolves, Ira?" Kezia asked him respectfully. With his harness on and his small jaw set, he truly looked like a soldier cat.

"Vicious, cunning animals that live in a pack. They are swift runners, and they kill not just to eat but also when the blood lust comes upon them. Or so said the soldiers under Gracus's command," Ira told her bluntly. "They would have killed us, too, if they had seen us. I ate too well of rich meat and slept, forgetting my duty. Gracus would have me court-martialed, I am sure." And Ira hung his head.

"But we are all safe," Abishag answered. "Except for the poor sheep—and Kezia and I will stand guard duty with you each night. We sleep sufficiently during the daytime travel anyway."

THE SAME SUNRISE found Gracus wakeful while on bivouac with a small contingent of men he was training. Although hundreds of miles away from them, Gracus had dreamed yet again of the three cats.

This is the day Polla and Citus are to take up residence in our new home. I shall ride back to the city tonight and surprise her. And I will ask her if she knows the significance of this dream.

POLLA COULD NOT help but stare as she rode in the cart with Citus, leaving the Roman legion encampment behind them. Zeugma, the city built on a steep hillside, which prospered mightily from the rich caravan trade and its river crossing, was certainly a sight at which to wonder.

"It is a strangely named city," she said to Citus.

"It means 'bridge' or 'crossroads' in the elders' form

of Greek," Citus answered her. "One of Alexander the Great's generals, Seleucus Nicator, founded it. How are you feeling? Is the jolting of the cart disturbing you?"

Although she was now visibly with child, she shook her head. "No, I am all right. Do we stop soon and camp, or what do we do?"

"Gracus wishes us to go to a house that he has now procured for you." Citus smiled at the surprise upon Polla's face. "See those large houses upon the hills that encircle the city? Gracus has selected a home so that you may be comfortable while you await the birth of his son."

Polla laughed. "And what if it is a daughter? Do I then assume my old tent?"

Citus shook his head. "You are going to be astonished at the beauty of your new home. The only material Zeugma lacks with which to build is marble. Without that, the artisans have resorted to crafting wondrous mosaics underfoot. When they need a certain color to finish a mosaic, if it is not readily procured from the gravel along the Euphrates, the artisans fashion stones of glass."

Gracious paths and ornately planted gardens beguiled them as they walked up the path to their new home. Once inside, Polla looked at Neptune riding in his golden chariot surrounded by other water gods and goddesses, the entire scene forming the bottom of a large pond ringed with columns set about it.

"What is this?"

"It is called a peristylium," Citus told her. "Notice how the figures seem to move, and how the light and shadows within the master craftsman's portrayal of the gods are perfectly balanced."

Polla sank down onto a bench alongside the wall. "And this large room, which brings gardens inside, is an atrium?"

"You add greatly to your vocabulary." Citus laughed.

"And so she should!" Gracus strode into the atrium and swept Polla up into his arms. "I have missed you while I have been on maneuvers. I fear the recruiting officers have somehow stumbled upon an entire field of donkeys turned into men, for these raw recruits are not trained at all. My little soldier knew more about drilling than I have yet been able to force into these stupid ones' heads!"

"Can you stay with us for the evening meal?" Polla asked eagerly.

"That is precisely why I have come, my heart."

While eating, Gracus told Polla of his assignment. "I shall be taking these new soldiers and hardening them by training them to protect the trade routes. But two days' ride away from the city the bandits prey upon the caravans."

"So you shall be teaching them in the midst of great danger to yourself." Polla sighed.

"I am a soldier," Gracus said simply. "I serve the emperor in whatever capacity he requests. But I have a question for you. Do you still believe the legends of your homeland, that women with child are also given the ability to read dreams?"

She nodded. "If not able to read dreams, we at least are often granted a sense of what is to come."

"Then tell me what you sense of this: I dreamed again of my little soldier; I could hear wolves howling in the blackness of night, but he did not seem afraid. And then time seemed to pass, but I know not whether it was days or weeks—he appeared in the daylight, and he had no limp." Gracus swallowed hard. "Does this mean he has died, and the gods have granted him immortality?"

Polla clasped her hands together. "Did he seem to come toward you?"

"Yes, I remember more of the dream now. He actually ran to me, and he limped no longer. I picked him up and heard him purr. And I marveled that his leg was straight once again."

Polla shook her head, and the thick blond braid swung as she did so. "The gods must have sent you this dream. I am sorry, but I cannot tell the meaning of it. If he has gone to a better place, perhaps with the gods somewhere, it is obvious he remembers you with love and admiration. What of the other two cats?"

"They were not in my dream." Now it was Gracus's turn to sigh. "He would not leave his foster sisters. My heart fears he is dead, perhaps killed by the wolves I heard howling."

Polla took Gracus's hand. "Then if this is true, he died a warrior's death, most probably defending his sisters."

"But what then has happened to the wise men?" Gracus asked her. "Have they all perished upon the journey to find the King they sought?"

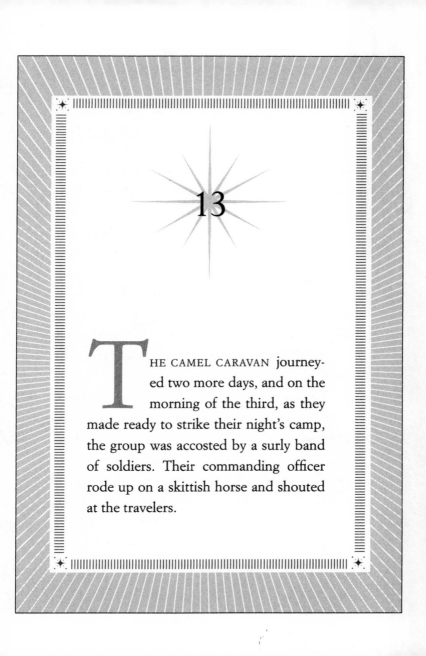

13

THE CAMEL CARAVAN journeyed two more days, and on the morning of the third, as they made ready to strike their night's camp, the group was accosted by a surly band of soldiers. Their commanding officer rode up on a skittish horse and shouted at the travelers.

"Whoever is deemed head of this crowd of trespassers, come forth! You are not within boundaries of the designated routes."

Kaspar looked at the other wise men, who nodded to him. The soldier's horse blew out its breath and danced about, frightened of the many camels, which were protesting and grumbling as the servants placed their packs and saddles upon them once again.

"I speak for us all," Kaspar said quietly. "And surely we do not trespass with intent to do so. We seek safe passage to Jerusalem, but we were set upon by wolves two nights past. We may have strayed from the route then, for we had to move our camp to protect the livestock."

"And what is your business in Jerusalem?" the officer demanded as he cleared his throat and spat. He had not even courteously dismounted while speaking to Kaspar. With a quick movement of his hand, he signaled his ragged group of foot soldiers to spread out along the edge of the camp while the servants finished preparing for the day's journey. Several of the men looked greedily at the packs, for here and there could be seen a glimpse of fine silks or tiny sparkles of jewelry.

"We seek the King of Kings," Kaspar said simply. "Have you heard word of His birth?"

"His birth? We have but one king, the king of Judea, and that is King Herod. You must pay us passage and then we shall escort you to him, so you may pay him homage. If you do not, we will imprison you and divide your goods among us. What will you?"

Balthazar stepped forward. "We bring gifts fit for your king," he assured the officer. "And passage money for those who serve him." He drew a leather pouch from a belt at his waist and opened it. Small gold coins fell out upon his palm as he shook the bag gently. He stepped up to the officer's horse and offered two gold coins to the man.

Next he swiftly walked to the foot soldiers and gave each of them one gold coin. Suspiciously, they bit the coins he had given them, and then their sullen faces showed surprise and pleasure at finding the coins genuine.

"Our passage is paid," Balthazar said.

"We will escort you to King Herod," the officer decided. "You are but one day's travel from his city, so you have only this night to camp upon the desert before you sleep in a palace." Laughing coarsely, he kicked his horse and gathered his men. They watched until the travelers were ready to leave, and then the officer rode to the head of the group while the foot soldiers brought up the rear.

Ira was appalled at the slovenly appearance of the soldiers and their equally dirty officer in command. *Even the horse's trappings are in poor condition,* he noted, watching the leader from his basket on Kaspar's camel. *None of them have bathed in weeks. They smell almost as bad as Asmodeus, by Mars.*

In camp that night, the three cats sat in a group so they could talk softly while on sentry duty. The city of Jerusalem was on the horizon, and small campfires dotted the desert landscape. Many other travelers—merchants, businessmen, slave traders, religious scholars, and pilgrims—were journeying to the city also.

"Who is this King Herod?" Kezia asked. "And why did the officer threaten Kaspar with imprisonment for all of us if they had no passage money?"

"I think they may not be actual soldiers in service to this King Herod they speak of," Ira said. "They resemble a band of brigands rather than military men. They are not Roman soldiers. I expect them to simply melt away, as the wolves did, once we are inside the city gates."

"As for Herod," Abishag said next. "He may well be the man Ptolemy called the 'false king.' We do know he is certainly not the one we seek."

"Well, I shall see a real palace at last," Kezia said. "But somehow things of that sort are beginning to seem less important. You know—" She paused. "I miss Gracus and Polla and Citus. But most of all, I am beginning to miss the ship and poor Alexos."

"What? Why?" Ira asked her, startled.

"You will think I am foolish. But Alexos thought I was the most intelligent, most beautiful cat he had ever seen. All because I killed that snake! He would slip tiny bits of delicacies to me after that. I tasted oyster and shrimp, mussel, and even rare abalone. If I fell asleep on his desk as he plotted the next day's course for the ship, he never pushed me roughly aside. Sometimes when I doze in my basket aboard Melchior's camel, I think I'm back on the ship . . ." Her voice trailed off, and Kezia looked dejected.

Abishag touched noses with her foster sister. "Why don't you plan on returning to Alexos, once we have completed our journey to see the Messiah?"

"But I would have to leave you two, if I did so."

Ira took a deep breath. "You would not be leaving me, for if the gods—or Ptolemy's One God, of Whom he taught us, permits, I wish to rejoin Gracus. I want to continue being a soldier; it is to my taste."

Abishag looked up at the star, which had grown huge in the eastern sky as they traveled these last weeks. She had already known the others did not wish to return to the tower. "We three will see the King of Kings," she said softly. "And then we three shall be parted, for I wish to return home."

"To Ptolemy," Kezia said. "Have you never realized he loves you?"

"He loves me as a daughter," Abishag told her.

"I don't think that's true," Ira said. "I saw his face

when you would enter our room at the tower. He always looked happier to see you than either of us."

Now it was Kezia's turn to reassure her sister. "Ira's right. You will be a good wife to Ptolemy. And even though he is old, he still may have many more years left."

Abishag sighed and began to wash her face with a paw.

"Thank you for your kind words. I, too, hope Ptolemy still lives, for I want to tell him of all we have seen and done." *I will not allow myself to hope he cares for me as I do for him,* she thought. *That hope must be set aside for the future.*

Carefully concealed in a pack, Asmodeus scratched a flea bite. *Well, I have no desire to return to that tower. But I hope I may never see another camel again in my life. Wretched creatures; they spit upon you when they are displeased— and when are they not?*

As the sun came up, the servants busied themselves with packs that had not yet been opened during the journey. Asmodeus had to desert his usual hiding places many times to avoid being caught by a human. Rich trappings for the camels were produced, and saddles were hung with tiny golden bells that rang sweetly with the beasts' movements. Beautiful, heavy robes with lavish embroidery and fur were pulled from the packs for the wise men, and their servants were dressed in bright colors of wool. Jewels twinkled from hands and chests. As their leather collars were gently removed and ropes of small pearls hung about their necks, Kezia and Abishag teased Ira about his obvious reluctance to part with the leather harness Citus had crafted for him.

"Come, little soldier," Kaspar said gently. "Do not hiss at me; you frightened my poor servant a moment ago. I will have your soldier's garb cleaned with saddle soap and carefully re-stitched while you match your sisters' finery and wear a gold chain as we enter the city."

Melchior chuckled. "He feels as foolish as we do in all this grandeur."

"But we must make an impression upon this king and win his regard if we are to be allowed passage to the Messiah," Balthazar said. "He rules not just Jerusalem, but all of Judea. And yet he began as a zealous tax collector."

"I heard he was valiant in battle," Melchior said. "And became a favored son of Rome by that means also."

A sumptuous procession entered Jerusalem upon that cold winter morning. People stood and stared, elbowing and pointing fingers for their neighbors to look also at the spectacle. Murmurs ran through the crowd: "They must be kings—only look how richly they are clothed!" "Even their servants are attired in wool and silk." "Not only servants—see the cage of doves—and is that cat wearing pearls?"

True to Ira's prediction, the motley group of soldiers had disappeared as the three wise men and their entourage entered the city. The black cat was glad to see real Roman soldiers just inside the gate, awaiting the travelers. *Clean and in uniform as soldiers should be,* he thought.

"In the emperor's name and that of King Herod, where do you travel and whom do you seek?" asked the gatekeeper.

"Hail to the emperor and also hail to King Herod," Kaspar began. "We seek an audience with King Herod, if it please him, for we have prophecies to relate and to verify with him."

A detachment of soldiers marched up then and quickly pushed aside the bystanders and foot traffic, opening the crowded road for the travelers. Six cavalrymen rode up and turned their mounts to lead the travelers to Herod's palace. "Follow these men," the gatekeeper ordered and returned to his post.

Oh, my, Kezia thought. *I often wished to see a procession such as this, and now I'm in one myself. What a strange world I have entered upon.*

Word of the visitors had of course been relayed with all haste to King Herod, and the heavily guarded gates to his palace stood open as they neared them. The contrast between the houses and walls of the city was startling, for the palace gleamed even at a distance with gold and inlaid tiles. A huge courtyard with a fountain many feet high could be seen as well, making the city about the palace seem drab and commonplace.

Once inside, the small caravan was greeted by King Herod's higher-ranking officials. Palace servants and slaves hurried to help the travelers dismount and offered delicate bowls of perfumed water and soft towels to dry their hands. They were then ushered to a wing of the huge building set aside especially for guests and visitors, or so they were informed by yet another official.

"May we speak with King Herod?" Kaspar asked.

"The king has not been well," the man answered. "I myself will ask his attendants to proffer your request to him. Meanwhile, please enjoy the comforts with which we have provided you." And he turned and left the main hall of the guests' wing.

"There is a feeling of deep sadness within this place," Melchior said softly, leaning toward his companions so he could not be overheard.

"It is an oppressive feeling, to my heart," Kaspar said. "We should not linger here, whether we are granted audience with King Herod or not."

Balthazar quietly gave orders to their servants to water the camels well and to remove the bells from their saddles.

"Also, except for the four of you who must accompany us, put away your own finery and lay out plain robes for us. Replace the cats' pearl necklaces with their leather collars, and return to the small soldier his leather harness. We shall leave immediately after whatever word comes from the king."

They settled themselves to wait.

To their surprise, within twenty minutes slippers could be heard slapping the marble floors of the corridor leading to their temporary quarters. The doves fluttered in their cage in fright as a slave ran into the room and prostrated himself at Kaspar's feet.

"King Herod bids you welcome, and to follow me to his rooms, for he has not been well, and does not wish to risk chilling himself."

The three men looked at one another, for the entire palace was overly warm, despite the winter winds.

"We are honored by his welcome," Melchior replied and raised the slave to his feet. "Why, you are but a boy!"

"I am in training for service to King Herod, king of the Jews," he answered. "And I have enough years to serve him well."

They had been offered subtle insult by Herod's officials having sent a mere slave lad to summon them to the presence of the king, but the men ignored the slight and began gathering their gifts.

Kaspar walked quickly to the cats' basket. "Stay here, little ones," he said softly. "This is a dangerous place for us all. When we return, we shall depart immediately." Ira looked up into Kaspar's face and quietly settled himself again in the basket, his foster sisters following suit.

Kaspar smiled at them. "You are good cats."

Two of their own servants carried the graceful golden cage with the three doves; another bore an intricately carved and inlaid wooden box in which the rings rested on silk; and the fourth carried a fortune's worth of unmounted jewels in a golden goblet. All followed the slave boy down the long hall.

They entered the stiflingly hot audience room, kept so with huge braziers laden with fiery coals in every corner. The three wise men bowed to the figure reclining upon a low bench with pillows heaped at one end.

"We bring greetings to you from lands that are many miles from here," Kaspar began.

Herod waved a hand. "I know you are visitors," his voice rasped. "What do you wish of me?"

Melchior stepped forward. "First, we wish to present you with some humble offerings, and then perhaps, if it does not tire you overly much, to speak with you about prophecies and other matters."

Herod's eyes gleamed at the thought of gifts, and he had of course already glimpsed the ornate birdcage. "Bring them forth." He popped several stuffed dates dripping with honey into his mouth.

The servant presented him with the goblet of jewels first. "A drink to toast your return to health," Kaspar

said, and Herod smiled slightly. He took the goblet with a hand that shook but still managed to pour out the gems upon a small table that stood nearby, and he sifted them through his sticky fingers.

"Truly, one could ransom a king with this many precious stones," Herod murmured.

Then Balthazar's servant stepped toward the ailing king. He opened the carved box and presented the rings. Herod frowned. "What are these? They are neither beautiful nor amazingly wrought."

Balthazar quickly related the story of how the rings had come to be found, and Herod's eyebrows worked themselves up into his hairline and remained there. "You found them by a dream's direction?"

"Yes, King Herod. And I know only that they must be precious in their application, for as you have said, they are but metal, stone, and wood."

"Hmm." Herod reached for the rings and put them on his left hand, not bothering to wash first. "Surely the metal one would belong to the finger of Jupiter and mighty rulers . . . and the one of stone would be for Saturn, having great responsibility . . . but that leaves the one of wood for the finger over which the heart rules." As Herod forced the wooden ring upon the third finger of his left hand, the ring broke in several pieces with a loud snap.

"Ah, what fortune!" Balthazar cried, thinking swiftly. "You see, King Herod, your heart is so strong, it has burst ordinary bonds! Whatever ails you, it must not be a disorder belonging to your chest."

Herod looked angry for a moment, but then considered what Balthazar had said. "Do you regard yourselves as prophets, then?" he asked silkily.

"In our own countries, we are revered as seers of the stars," Kaspar told him, and he beckoned the servants carrying the doves forward. Herod peered into the cage. The birds cooed and tilted their small heads, gazing back at the man looking at them. He felt the gold bars, and his lips moved as he began to count the many jewels entwined therein.

When he reached fifty, he sighed and settled back among his pillows. "This is the most richly wrought cage I have yet beheld," he muttered. "You may take the boy who guided you here with you when you leave, as my thanks."

The three wise men bowed again. Then Kaspar spoke.

"It is we who must thank you for your gift to us of your slave. But, King Herod, we still wish to ask you of ancient prophecies. We have traveled to your country to seek the one they call the Messiah."

"What need have you of my thoughts, when you yourselves study the stars?" he growled. Then he snapped his fingers. "You, boy! Bring my chief priests and scribes here." Grudgingly, he bade them be seated and had another servant offer the wise men some of the honeyed dates.

Within moments, six or seven elderly men assembled in the room. When Herod challenged them as to whether a new Messiah had been born, they gasped and mumbled and appeared extremely distressed. Herod pressed them again.

"Your reactions tell me that there has indeed been something said of this. Tell me quickly, or you shall . . ." He remembered his guests and turned toward them. "Please allow these learned men to quarrel among themselves until they reach consensus."

A few moments later, the youngest, though still with white hair and beard, stepped toward King Herod and bowed. "We know of some prophecies, but we think the one to which these men refer must be that of Micah. It is hundreds of years old."

"And it tells of what?" Herod asked.

"The location of the birth of the Messiah."

Herod's face turned gray, and his mouth sagged open.

"The location of the *birth*?" he repeated incredulously. "Of the Messiah? What Messiah?"

"The Jews expect a Messiah, the King of the Jews, the King of Kings, to be born, who will return their lands to them and then rule over all the earth."

Herod shuddered. Then he turned to the three wise men, and his eyes glittered with malice. "Are you Jews?"

"No, we are but astronomers," Melchior said quickly. "We have been following an unusual star and thought to ask you, the most learned man in these parts, whether the ancient prophecies concerned it."

Herod thought for several long moments, while the three men waited. *He shall surely have us put to death,* Kaspar thought. Melchior and Balthazar watched the king closely.

"Tell me the prophecy." Herod turned to his priests, reaching for the honeyed dates again.

The same aged man stepped forward. *"But you, Bethlehem Ephrathah, though you are little among the thousands of Judah, yet out of you shall come forth to Me the One to be Ruler in Israel, whose goings forth have been from old, from everlasting."* He recited from memory.

Silence in the room was broken only by the sounds of a few coals hissing.

Suddenly a coughing spell shook Herod's body, and he gasped for breath. Servants ran to him, one with a flagon of vinegar, some with goblets of water or wine, while others ran toward the doors to summon help.

Melchior leaped to his feet and ran to Herod. He struck the king between his shoulder blades, expelling a date pit from Herod's mouth.

Herod drew in a gasp of air, and then shakily gulped down a goblet of wine. "As you see, I am an ill man. I thank you for saving my life and ask only that when you find this Messiah, you return and tell me of him. Although I wish to do so, I cannot accompany you because of my precarious health." He held out his goblet to be refilled and drank deeply again. "As king, I must know all that occurs in my country, and I would not neglect to proclaim a birth of such ancient importance. I only hope he is not a man already, with me unknowingly slighting his rulership." He waved a hand at the slave boy and, while handing him the empty goblet, hissed, "Go with them, and return to me. And be sure you recall to me exactly where they find this pretender to the throne. If you do not remember where I may find this—Messiah—I will cut out your tongue."

Kaspar, Melchior, and Balthazar hurriedly made their

farewells and left the room, taking the ashen-faced slave with them.

The official who had met them originally was waiting for them in the guest quarters. "And what have you discussed with King Herod?" he asked.

"We have been given a task," Kaspar answered. "We are to find the newborn Messiah and then return to bring the news to King Herod, for he has said this is our duty. And as you see, we make haste to obey the king."

Within the hour and while some daylight lingered, they had left not only the palace but Jerusalem as well.

Balthazar shook his head at the events of the past few hours. *Servants and slaves whisper rumors of Herod's own sons, whom he put to death to prevent their ascension to his throne. That ring must have broken from the hardness of Herod's heart.* He and the others were riding swiftly across the desert as the cold wind grew more bitter and snow began to fly.

"I would far rather be out here in this storm than in that overly warm palace!" he called to the other men. They nodded in agreement, glad to be out of Herod's clutches. But the small slave boy they had been given shut his eyes and clung in genuine terror to the servant mounted in front of him, for he had never before seen a camel, much less ridden upon one.

What do we do now? Abishag wondered. And then she knew. *We follow the star, of course.* And she slept peacefully in her basket.

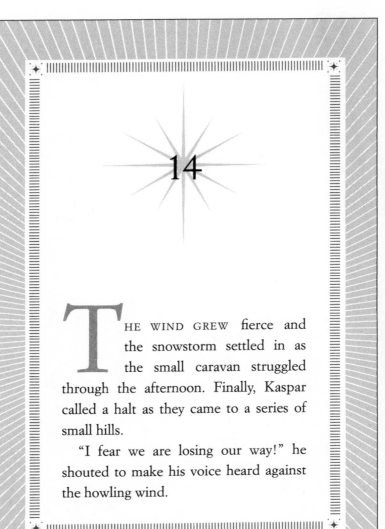

14

THE WIND GREW fierce and the snowstorm settled in as the small caravan struggled through the afternoon. Finally, Kaspar called a halt as they came to a series of small hills.

"I fear we are losing our way!" he shouted to make his voice heard against the howling wind.

Balthazar turned in his saddle. Cupping his hands about his mouth, he shouted in return, "Let us make camp here and wait for the storm to cease!"

Wiping ice crystals from his face, Melchior leaned over Kezia's basket. "Are you faring well, small one? We shall have a cold camp tonight, I believe, but surely this storm cannot last much longer."

Unable to keep even a small fire going in the icy blasts, the wise men placed the cats' big basket in the middle of the camels' circle as the beasts rested. They had their servants wrap up warmly, as they did themselves, and all settled to wait out the ferocious storm, backs to the small bluffs for scant protection.

The storm lingered until after noon the next day. Drifts of snow and ice crystals had sifted over the backs of the camels and glittered upon the packs. Throughout the storm, the three men had checked on their servants and animals, not forgetting to remind Herod's slave boy to rise and stamp his feet periodically. The camels had been fed, but everyone else felt hunger along with the cold. Finally Balthazar managed to get some wisps of kindling burning and carefully added bits of charcoal to a small brazier.

Kaspar nudged him as they watched the small curl of smoke. "And what did we say not one day past about an overly heated palace?"

Balthazar chuckled. "Had we had but two of Herod's huge braziers, we would have had a feast in the midst of the blizzard."

Scrambling out of their basket, the cats remembered to thank the camels for sharing their warmth during the bitter cold. Then they followed Ira to the small hills.

"I don't really know whether they understand us or not," Abishag said thoughtfully. "They may not speak cat."

"But it's always best to remember your manners," Kezia said. "Why are we traveling to the hills?"

"There may be something to eat there," Ira answered. "I cannot wait until Kaspar and his servants get something cooked to eat; my stomach is complaining more loudly than my ears can stand now!"

They dug out a few odd-looking beetles from the ice under the branches of a small bush, but just as they were about to eat them, Asmodeus called.

"There is a mouse hole with several occupants over by that far stone. May I have the beetles?"

Ira blinked. "You are still with us?"

"Yes, and I have just found your meal for you," the rat said. "Does that not give me the quality of being an agreeable companion?"

"I wouldn't say that," Abishag answered. "But you may have the beetles."

Each cat had a small mouse and then they went back to the campsite to warm themselves at the fire that had been built. The weak daylight showed the three wise men crouched about a map Balthazar had drawn in the sand, now wet from the snow melt.

"Have we actually become lost?" Melchior asked.

"No, I think we cannot be truly lost," Kaspar said. "But we shall wait until the star rises this night to once again determine our route. The distance from Jerusalem to Bethlehem is short; a man could walk it in a day. That storm prevented us from reaching the small town as early as my heart urged. So we must spend tonight upon the desert also."

As the camp settled for the night, the star they had been following for so very long rose, and then it seemed to remain still in front of them. Its radiance streamed from it in pulsating waves, filling the very sky with the scintillating colors of jewels. Kaspar, Balthazar, and Melchior stood, the starlight lighting their faces and showing their tears of joy.

"The miracle unfolds!" Kaspar said, his voice shaking, and he fell to his knees upon the snow-drifted desert sand. All the servants, the cats, even the sheep and camels raised their heads, staring in awe at the heavenly beacon.

"Surely the Messiah has been born," Melchior murmured, as he and Balthazar knelt in prayer with Kaspar.

How long they prayed, moments or hours, they never knew; they were only recalled to earthly matters by the sounds of sheep bleating in the darkness about them.

"There are several flocks of wandering sheep that seem to have no shepherd with them," a servant reported. "Shall we try to herd them with our few?"

"That is odd," Melchior said thoughtfully. "Perhaps they were lost during that ferocious storm. Yes, gather them as best you can, for even on such a wondrous night there may be wolves and other creatures lurking."

"We are so near our journey's end," Balthazar marveled. "I cannot sleep."

Nor could the rest of the camp for that night. Servants reclined upon packs, unwilling to take their eyes from the most stupendous sight anyone had ever before seen.

The three cats watched with the rest, Abishag wishing Ptolemy had traveled with them to see the marvel.

"I wonder if Alexos has seen this star and uses it to guide his ship," Kezia whispered.

"Or if Gracus has seen it while out on maneuvers with his troops," Ira added.

"I shall be very glad when we can ask our friends and loved ones those very questions," Abishag replied and tucked her paws underneath her as she rested atop a pack.

The next morning's breakfast was hasty, as they wished to rush to the end of their journey. Just as they began to urge the camels to rise with their packs and saddles, a group of shepherds rushed up to them.

"You have our sheep!" one shouted. "Stop, thieves!"

Kaspar immediately got out of his saddle. "No, we are not thieves. We found your flocks wandering without guidance, and kept them with our animals for the night."

An older shepherd pulled the arm of the one who had shouted, and forced him back. "Please pardon his rude words, sir. We left our sheep to follow a star, and saw—" The man's dirt-smudged, bearded face suddenly glowed. He paused and began again. "We have seen the Messiah!"

The three wise men gathered around the ragged, dirty shepherds. "You have seen Him! Where is He? May we go to Him?"

"He lies in a manger, in a stable not far from here. The stable is on the outskirts of Bethlehem," the older man continued.

"In a manger? It is true He is but a babe, then?" Balthazar asked incredulously.

"But He is born to be King of the Jews," another shepherd offered. "For last night we did see angels, who took us to Him."

"Angels," Kaspar repeated. "What wonders we should have seen. If only the storm had not delayed us so!"

A small boy walked up then. "You will see the angels, too," he told the wise men shyly. "For they fly over the stable as they sing."

"And what songs we heard!" The voices of the shepherds tumbled over one another as they each tried to be heard. "They were glorious!" "That is what they were singing: Glory, glory, glory to God! On earth peace, and goodwill toward men." "They filled the sky with their wings and voices and music!" "We heard voices that sounded more sweetly than any bells could ring."

Time passed as the shepherds tried to speak of the wonders they had seen and heard. Finally the sheep were given back to the care of their shepherds, and the three wise men set off upon the last few hours of their journey once again. Abishag could hardly stand to remain in her basket; she wanted to run and leap and dance at the news the shepherds had brought.

A crowd upon the highway leading to the small town slowed the camels' usual pace to a very slow walk. Some people walked, many rode in wagons or on small donkeys, but all hastened toward Bethlehem. The cold wind began again and brought with it bits of sleet that stung everyone's faces.

"What is this sudden influx of people?" Balthazar asked, leaning from his saddle and asking a man walking nearby.

"We must register and pay our taxes to the emperor," the man told him. "Are you ignorant of the laws?"

"I fear I am," Balthazar answered. "I am a stranger in these lands, as are my companions."

The man scowled at the small caravan and hastened on.

As they neared the outskirts, they realized there were many small buildings and stables in which the Messiah might have been born. Kaspar asked a servant to seek information from the owner of the first inn they found.

"May I speak with your master?" the servant asked a slave who had opened the door. But he was never allowed inside, for the innkeeper, Jethro Ben Solomon, shouted at his slave. "Quit talking and close the door! We have no more room, and the wind is stealing the warmth from the fire!"

"But, master, there are rich customers here—" the slave began. He had seen the rich clothing the servant wore.

"Close the door!" the innkeeper bellowed, and Kaspar's servant drew back as the door was slammed shut. "You stupid slave," Ben Solomon grumbled. "Do you always open the door so the little warmth we have flees into the cold? Two nights past you wanted me to take in that beggar couple with the lame donkey. And now you pretend these travelers are rich men. I should have you whipped!"

The travelers wound through the streets of Bethlehem Ephrathah, searching for the one stable in which the King of Kings had been born. The wind was driving the chill into everyone's bones when evening fell—and the glorious star rose once again.

"There!" shouted Melchior, and he pointed as the magnificent star came to rest directly above a small stable.

As the caravan halted, the innkeeper himself came to the door. "Good evening, gentlemen," Timothy Ben David greeted the three wise men. "I regret that I have no more rooms left for such esteemed visitors."

"We are able to care for ourselves, if you will permit us to stay within the walls of your courtyard," Kaspar told him. "But may we give our camels water?"

"Stay, and welcome. And of course you must give your animals water," Ben David said. "Do you need food?"

Melchior dismounted and walked over to the innkeeper.

"We have brought our own, but we wish to pay you for allowing us to remain here within your outer walls for a time." He held out a small bag of gold coins to Ben David.

"That is too much," the innkeeper said. "Before I even open the bag, there are too many coins in it for but a place to camp. I cannot accept such overpayment."

Balthazar walked up then. "Please, you would dishonor us and the One we seek should you refuse our offering."

"Whom do you seek?"

"We seek the Messiah, who is a newborn babe, as we have been told."

"There is but one newborn babe here, and he is with his parents in my stable, for I had not even a corner inside my walls to give them for lodging. If it is he you seek, then you have found him. How brightly shines the moon this night! I had not thought it to be full just yet."

"We have indeed found Him." Kaspar nodded, and he nudged his camel to lie down so he could in turn dismount.

Melchior pressed the bag of coins into Ben David's hand, who protested again, then finally accepted the money and went back into his inn.

"He does not know of the prophecies, nor has he seen the star," Balthazar whispered incredulously to the other wise men.

"Even good men see only what their eyes are prepared to see," Kaspar said. "But now, let us find our gifts for the Messiah and make haste to greet Him."

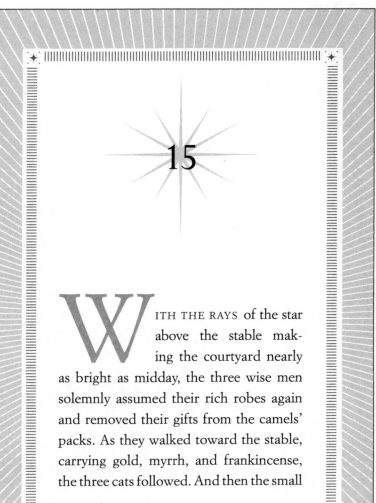

15

WITH THE RAYS of the star above the stable making the courtyard nearly as bright as midday, the three wise men solemnly assumed their rich robes again and removed their gifts from the camels' packs. As they walked toward the stable, carrying gold, myrrh, and frankincense, the three cats followed. And then the small procession stumbled to a halt, as the heavens suddenly opened around the star and showed rank upon rank of angels, singing and rejoicing in magnificent voices that resounded with sweetness.

"Blessed is He!" Kaspar gasped and fell to his knees, looking up into the angels' faces as they hovered above the lowly stable. The cats bowed their heads, then raised them to look with wonder at an angelic cat, perched upon the roof of the stable.

Melchior knelt trembling, and for a moment, dared not raise his eyes. Tears streamed down his face, running unnoticed to his chin when he finally looked up to behold the heavenly choir. And Balthazar sobbed as he repeated under his breath the prayers of his ancestors.

The angels smiled and continued their glorious songs, raising their hands in blessing as men and cats slowly walked to the stable door.

Softly the men knocked on the door frame, and then a low voice bade them enter. The cats hesitated on the threshold.

"Are we—are we allowed to see the Messiah also?" Ira, his voice trembling, asked the angelic cat.

The large black cat leaned closer to its earthly siblings. "Of course you may," he said. "You may see and worship the Messiah as we have all come to do this glorious night. And do not be afraid of me, for I am your guardian angel. My name is Charko, and I have been with you, unseen, during this long journey."

"That is why we have had such help from all humans!" Abishag cried. "It has been as if we spoke in a language they understood."

"Hearts always speak the same language," Charko told her gently.

"But how is it we could not see you before?" Kezia whispered.

"You are now in a place of miracles. Go in and see the babe, the King of Kings."

As they entered the old building, time seemed to sigh and then stop. The three wise men knelt on the stable floor, their faces filled with love and wonder as they gazed at the babe asleep on His mother's lap.

When He stirred in His sleep, Joseph quietly asked Mary if she wanted to place the baby in the manger once again. She rose and started to walk a step or two, carrying her newborn babe, but halted as a huge dog raised its head from the manger and snarled.

Ira was upon the dog before the brute knew what had attacked him. "Get out!" Scratching and hissing, Ira drove the dog, four times his size, from the sweet-smelling hay.

Mary held the babe tightly until the dog, growling and threatening still, slunk away, and then lowered Him gently to the rough bed.

"Thank you," she said to Ira and sat down once again, close to the manger. The wise men spoke to her and to Joseph then, keeping their voices low so as not to disturb the babe. They offered their gifts to His earthly parents.

"We realize He, as a babe, has no need of these things now," Kaspar said, "but please use them as you see fit for Him." Mary smiled, and Kaspar felt himself blessed beyond ordinary men.

"Your coming was foretold to me," she said simply. "Will you not tell me of the journey you undertook?"

As the wise men continued to marvel at being in the very presence of the King of Kings, and to speak of their travels, the air grew colder within the small stable. The babe frowned in His sleep, and Kezia noticed. She nudged Ira and Abishag.

"We must keep Him from getting chilled," she whispered to the others. "Those swaddling clothes don't look very warm to me." She jumped up into the hay, landing lightly so as not to wake the babe. She settled herself into the hay, carefully tucking His tiny toes and feet beneath her thick, warm fur. Abishag leaped up into the manger and snuggled close to His left side as Ira did the same on the babe's right. They all purred, and the babe sighed softly, sleeping soundly once more.

All had watched as the cats made the babe's bed warm in the frigid temperature. Joseph smiled and put his hand on Mary's shoulder.

"You need not worry about Him being cold tonight,"

he told her, and she reached over and stroked each cat's head.

The wise men then shrugged out of their heavy cloaks and insisted Mary and Joseph take them to keep out the fierce cold.

Asmodeus crept out of the pack in which he had traveled and ran toward the stable. Blinded by the wind, he ran against the dog's side as the huge beast lay sullenly outside the door.

"A rat!" The dog sprang to his feet and snarled. "Good; I can kill you now and get back in their good graces."

"My dear dog," Asmodeus began, trying to talk himself out of yet another dangerous encounter. "Do not, I implore you, dispatch me with such haste."

"What?"

"What is your name, good dog?"

"Goliath. Why should you care who kills you?" And Goliath opened his jaws, showing the rat his teeth.

"Why would you devour the one who can help you plan punishment for the cats? The cats who caused you to be turned out of your warm, soft bed?"

"Talk fast, then." And a whispered conversation took

place between the rat and the dog, unheard by the cats, who had dozed off beside the tiny Messiah.

It was near dawn before the wise men finished speaking with Mary and Joseph and turned to leave the stable.

"We should not have tired you so with our tales," Kaspar began, as he realized how exhausted the new mother looked. Mary shook her head.

"I can sleep at other times," she said. "And look, your good cats have kept our son warm throughout the night."

"Truly, they have had the privilege of being a living blanket for the Messiah," Melchior agreed.

"Now we must see to our servants and camels," Balthazar said. "And we must return to our homes soon, to tell all who will listen of the Messiah's birth."

They left the cats and babe still sleeping together in the hay and quietly returned to the small, muddy courtyard.

Midmorning, Mary and Joseph dozed upon a thin pallet of straw in the corner, the cloaks pulled over them. The cats woke, started to scramble from the hay—and realized the babe was watching them.

"We did not mean to wake You," Abishag told Him, contritely.

In answer, the babe laughed and stretched out His small hands. He touched Kezia, and she gently licked the tiny fingers.

When He touched Ira, there was a soft snapping sound, and the small soldier gasped. "My leg! My leg— it's straight again!"

And Abishag cried out to Kezia, "Your ear! It's perfect once more!"

"How can we ever thank You?" Kezia asked the babe, who only smiled.

The three cats ran to the wise men, who rubbed their eyes and stared at them dancing about and purring loudly in the courtyard.

"We have witnessed His first miracles," Balthazar said. "Indeed He is the Son of the One God."

"How could He have done these things?" the slave boy Herod had sent with them asked. "He is but a babe."

"He is the Messiah, the Son of God," Melchior told him.

Asmodeus watched the cats capering and snorted.

"Are they suffering from delusions? What are they so happy about?" He suddenly saw Ira's legs. "What has happened to his crooked leg? The one the centurion's horse nearly crushed." He stared at Ira, then noticed Kezia's ear. "Now my good eye must be losing its vision, for I would swear she has two perfect ears upon her head once more!"

Asmodeus dashed across the length of the courtyard and into the stable. *Whatever has healed them came about in this place. And it must have something to do with the humans who are staying here.* Panting, he crouched under the manger. Hearing the babe laugh, the rat crept out from under the improvised cradle and crawled up onto the hay.

He reached out His small hand and touched

the very tip of Asmodeus's nose. Afraid, the rat jerked his head back and fell out of the manger and onto the hard dirt floor. Stunned, he shook his head and then opened his eyes. His jaw dropped, and he put his paws up to his mouth. "My eyes! I can see again! My teeth— they're not broken—and even my tail!"

He whirled and looked back up at the babe. "Who are You?" Asmodeus asked wonderingly. "How can You do such miracles?" He turned to leave, turned back. "Thank You."

Goliath met him outside the door. "When are we going to kill the cats as we planned?"

Asmodeus gasped. "I—er—we must wait," he babbled. He thought quickly, still stunned by the restoration of his broken body. "The humans must not guess what we plan, for they would put us to death

instead. In three days' time, we should be able to safely rid the stable of the cats. Forever."

Two more days passed, and the wise men knew in their hearts that they must be starting homeward. They told the servants to pack things for the journey, to check saddles and secure initial provisions for the long trip home.

"We will say our farewells," Kaspar said that night as they left their campfire in the courtyard to go and see the babe once more.

Mary smiled upon them, and Joseph clasped their hands in his own, roughened by years of carpentry.

"We thank you for your many kindnesses, large and small. Now we find you paid for our stay here at the inn, and you have given our donkey, Gideon, good grain with a richly embroidered nosebag from which to eat it."

The wise men knelt then, and worshipped the babe one final time, even though they were sad at the departure. When they returned to the courtyard, the cats hurried into the stable and leaped into the hay. He blessed them silently as each cat gently licked His small hand, purred thanks, and left.

"And what of the slave boy Herod gave us?" Balthazar asked Kaspar quietly, before they all slept for a few hours. "I believe Herod charged him with bringing news to him of the Messiah. My heart aches when I think of this, for I fear Herod means to do Him harm while He is but a babe."

"I, too, have the same fear," Melchior said, joining the quiet conversation, out of earshot of the young slave. "Should we insist he remain with us?"

"No," Kaspar said slowly. "We shall simply revert to our generous natures and give the boy his own camel with which to return to Herod."

Balthazar and Melchior laughed silently until they clutched their sides. "By the time he learns to control that camel, the Messiah and His family will be safely on their way to Nazareth," Melchior sputtered.

"And we shall be safely out of Herod's clutches also," Balthazar gasped. "Kaspar, you are a rogue."

"So says my kinsman, Alexos, the sea captain. I shall be glad to see him at the docks of Tyre once more."

Kezia stood beside the small heap of readied packs in the courtyard, her heart hammering. *Alexos! He is speaking of Alexos—and we are going to meet him again! Oh, blessed be His name, for I believe He has caused this unforeseen chance to return to my captain!*

She ran to tell the other two cats.

"Wonderful news, foster sister," Ira congratulated her. "I will pray to return to Gracus."

"And I shall pray to return home," Abishag said happily.

At dawn the next day, the three wise men left the courtyard with heavy hearts, for they knew something of the terrible tribulations that would beset the Messiah in His future life. "Since He is the One God's Son, perhaps He will somehow be safe from the evil of men," Kaspar murmured as they rode slowly into the dusty street.

Asmodeus watched them leave. He had gathered rich, fatty mutton bones discarded the night before from camps and kitchens and fed Goliath well, thinking the vicious dog would then sleep through the caravan's departure.

As her camel turned to go around the gatepost and leave the courtyard, Abishag looked out of her basket and saw Asmodeus. "What, are you staying?" she called to him.

"Yes. I wish to serve Him now. So I must follow Him to wherever His life leads," the rat called in return. He nodded to the black cat. The very last camel, bearing the terrified slave boy, left the courtyard.

A large shadow fell across him from behind, and Asmodeus caught his breath.

"It's the third day, and the cats are gone. Not killed," Goliath growled.

"Yes. They are on their way, safe from your jaws," Asmodeus replied and suddenly dashed into the stable, inches ahead of Goliath's teeth. He ran to the manger and jumped up into the hay at the babe's feet. He was awake and looked at the rat with interest.

"I ask Your pardon," the rat said softly. "I am not worthy to be here, not even at Your small feet. But I would thank You again, for restoring me to robust health. And—and surely there is some small way in which I may serve You? Perhaps I might keep spiders or beetles from disturbing You?" He clasped his paws together.

The babe laughed, and tears of joy stood in Asmodeus's eyes. "Soon Your parents must return to Nazareth, for I have heard them speak of this. Please, let me accompany You. For my heart tells me that even a rat may serve the King of Kings."

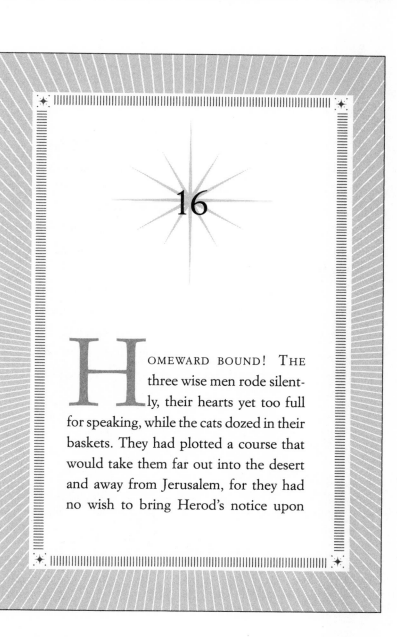

16

HOMEWARD BOUND! THE three wise men rode silently, their hearts yet too full for speaking, while the cats dozed in their baskets. They had plotted a course that would take them far out into the desert and away from Jerusalem, for they had no wish to bring Herod's notice upon them again. The slave boy continued to struggle with his stubborn young camel.

They slipped past the last turning toward the city and rode another hour. Then they spoke to the slave boy.

"We think you would be unhappy in our homelands, for they are far from here," Melchior began.

"And the only means of transport is of course by camel," Balthazar added. The slave boy shuddered and nearly fell from his saddle.

"If you ride straight toward the sun, you will return to your former master," Kaspar added. "You should be at his palace gates before two days have passed." And he slapped the camel upon its rump, causing the beast to leap suddenly and almost seem to fly over the desert floor.

Balthazar shaded his eyes. "I vow we never attained such speed before upon that particular animal's back."

"At least he is traveling in the correct direction," Melchior said. "Imagine his surprise when he rides into Jerusalem before nightfall!"

The caravan itself did not stop that night, nor did it stop the next day for long. Feeding and watering the camels, with but quick breaks for themselves and the cats, the three wise men made haste toward the west and safety from Herod's wrath.

THE SLAVE BOY managed to stay in the saddle and return to the outskirts of Jerusalem. The moment his uncontrollable camel was spotted galloping across the desert, Roman soldiers rode out to meet the boy. Sentries had been watching each day for any sign of the returning caravan, for Herod craved news of the three wise men and their search for the Messiah—or so he said.

Quickly subduing the camel, soldiers pulled the slave from his saddle and marched the boy to Herod's palace.

Once the slave was inside the walls, he was astonished, for the king actually strode from his overheated rooms to demand of him, "Well? And did they find this new King of the Jews?"

"They did," he gasped, still breathing hard from his forced march through the streets of Jerusalem.

"And you can show my soldiers the palace in Bethlehem where he sits upon his throne?"

"There is no palace in Bethlehem! It is but a small, humble, lowly town, with buildings of the meanest materials. And He sits upon no throne, but lies in a manger filled with hay for His crib."

Herod stared at the boy until he ceased gasping and began to tremble. "Do you mock me, boy?"

"No, I would not, King Herod. I would never mock you in any fashion!"

The king stood deep in thought until his legs began to weaken from the unaccustomed exertion, and he sat down in a litter chair, summoned to him by a mere snap of his fingers.

"Then you shall take soldiers with you and direct them to the place where this babe lies in a certain stable. And they will carry out my orders. You have done well, boy. What is your name?"

"Thomas."

"Go and sleep with the soldiers tonight then, Thomas. Soon you depart, to lead them to the—Messiah." Laughing, Herod raised his hand and his chair was lifted up and bore him away to his overheated rooms once more.

On his way to the soldiers' barracks, Thomas's heart jumped in his chest and he staggered as a premonition grew in his mind. *King Herod means to kill the babe! He doesn't want a king who might replace him—did he not murder his own sons to save his throne? Herod will have his soldiers kill the babe and parents, too. I can't lead the soldiers to that stable. The wise men said the babe is truly the newborn Messiah. I do not know that for myself. But I—I must somehow return to the wise men. They will know what to do.*

Thomas turned to the soldiers as they saw the barracks doors ahead of them. "May I have my camel again?"

"Why would you, a foolish slave boy, have need of a camel in Jerusalem?" one of the soldiers answered.

"I want to sell him, so I may have money."

"Money for what?" another soldier asked.

"To gamble. I am very lucky at games of chance."

The first soldier's eyes gleamed beneath his helmet.

"Are you? Then go, and sell your camel! Hasten back here, and I myself will play a friendly game or two with you. Be sure you get a good price for the camel."

"Oh, I will. His saddle will bring a good price, too."

FOUR DAYS OUT into the desert, the three wise men began to feel a little easier in their minds. On the fourth night, they stopped and made camp, easing the packs and saddles from the tired and grumbling camels at last. The cats, too, were so tired they could barely crawl from their baskets.

"I think I have bruises under my fur from rattling around in that basket all this time," Kezia grumbled. "Alexos had better have some especially tasty treat for me when I return to his ship."

"I only hope I may somehow find Gracus." Ira sighed as he finished scratching his back. Then he shook the loose dirt from his fur, setting his foster sisters sneezing.

"Ira! Must you always do that!" Kezia began to scold him. Then she stopped and looked at the black cat beside her. "Oh! I just realized—this is the last journey we will all have together."

Abishag nodded, sinking down upon a pack, too tired even to wash her small face. "Yes, for you will go to sea as soon as we find Alexos. And I am sure Ira will somehow be reunited with Gracus. I will miss you two very much when I am at home; that is, if the Messiah will help me to return." She licked a sore spot upon her paw.

The weary caravan rested the next day and night also, for when the servants tried to load the camels' packs upon their backs again, the great beasts snort-ed and showed their teeth, refusing to stand.

"They are wiser than we are," Kaspar told the servants. "We, too, need rest. And we shall do so today."

Late that afternoon, Balthazar suddenly stood and shouted, "A camel! One lone camel—and one rider. It is the slave boy Herod gave us!"

The camel came slowly into the camp, grumbling a greeting to the other camels as it recognized them. Thomas was exhausted, slumped over the beast's neck, and Kaspar felt heartsick as he gently lifted the boy from his saddle. Black circles were under his eyes, and he begged for food and water.

Melchior had a servant tend to the weary young camel and dipped a large bowl of good hearty soup from the kettle over the fire.

Thomas gulped at the soup and then closed his eyes, only to sit up suddenly. "You must know! King Herod wanted me to go back with soldiers to Bethlehem and show them where the babe was. But I slipped out of Jerusalem after my camel rested a few hours. How I found you, I do not know. But I dare not return to Herod now."

"Indeed you shall not," Kaspar told him. "And I owe you an apology, for it was I who insisted you must return to the king, and on camelback. You have done well. Will you come with me to Athens? I wish to grant you your freedom, and to offer you a home as well."

Thomas had tears in his eyes, and he
sniffled. "I will come with you willingly.
For I wish to learn more of this Messiah. It
was He I asked, as we ran through the days
and nights, to guide me to you, for I had no
idea where to find you in this vast desert."

Dawn came, and a cold wind whistled from
the north as they broke camp and rode out upon
the desert once more. Suddenly the air was filled
with shouts and curses, and the small caravan
looked back to see bandits riding fast horses across
the desert. Wicked sword blades glittered in the early
sunlight, and Kaspar shouted to his servants, "Stay
together; do not fall behind! If one camel slows, we all
slow. We ride together or we ride separately to a sure
death!"

Then began a desperate dash across the sandy soil.
Their hired guards were too few to defend against such
numbers of brigands. The camels at first seemed to have
the advantage, for their feet were adapted to the sand
far better than the hooves of the horses, but they were
still tired from their forced journey of the previous days.
Ira looked out from his basket and gritted his teeth,

watching the horses gaining on them. *They must be a gang of desert marauders. They may have followed us for days, waiting for us to tire, or perhaps they merely lie in wait for unlucky travelers. Only Roman soldiers could save us now, and how are they to find us in time?* He thought of the Messiah and silently sent a prayer to Him, asking for rescue to come, somehow.

And come it did, for from behind a series of low hills came legionnaires marching, banners and plumes waving in the bitterly cold air. The bandits, seeing the soldiers, began yanking on their horses' reins, trying to turn the galloping beasts before they could bring their riders within range of the Romans' weapons. Ira yowled an exuberant greeting to the soldiers, even knowing full well they couldn't hear him.

The caravan raced down a small hill and finally got the camels calmed to a walk. "We shall make camp here tonight!" Kaspar called, his chest heaving from the mad ride across the desert.

"Thank the Messiah for sending us succor!" Melchior called to his companions and slid from his saddle before his camel had fully knelt. "How glad my heart will be to see my home in Alexandria once more!"

The members of the caravan turned in time to watch as a volley of Roman arrows found their marks, and seventeen of the band of cutthroats died in their saddles. The other thieves screamed horribly and beat their tired horses with whips, riding back over the far crest of the small hills and disappearing from view. Ira leaped from his basket and danced in the sand. "Well done, men! Well done!"

He raced over to the packs as soon as they were stacked and clambered upon them, the better to watch the soldiers as they regrouped and marched toward the camp. A chariot and driver joined them, the driver's plumed helmet nodding as the commander congratulated his young men on their successful rout of the bandits.

And then, as the centurion began driving closer to the camp, something about the man seemed familiar to Ira. He stretched his neck to its limit, trying to see yet farther. Quickly he licked a paw and rubbed it across his face and tried to calm his pounding heart. *It can't be! But it is! Thank You, Messiah! Thank You!*

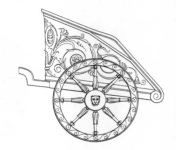

As the gleaming silver chariot entered the camp, Ira leaped from the packs and dashed toward the vehicle. The centurion handed his reins to another soldier and turned to speak to the man he assumed was the caravan leader.

Gracus stared and removed his helmet, to run his hand through his thick hair in his usual gesture. "Can it indeed be Alexos's kinsman, Kaspar of Athens?"

Then the centurion's face turned white, for Ira ran straight up to him, stopped, and held up his left leg, turning his paw in a salute.

"My little soldier!" he gasped. "I feared you dead!" And he stooped and gathered Ira into his arms, not caring whether that was dignified behavior for a Roman centurion. Ira purred as loudly as he could and licked Gracus's face with his rough tongue.

A short distance away, Kezia and Abishag watched, lumps in their throats as they saw Ira greet the man who was his true friend and comrade.

"So Ira will be a soldier once more," Kezia said softly. "I certainly hope Gracus has another harness made for him; that one is too shabby for words, even if Kaspar did have it cleaned and repaired." And she sniffed, but whether from disdain or a full heart, Abishag couldn't tell.

That night around the campfire, the ordinary stars saw the members of the caravan and the soldiers trading tales, enjoying each other's company.

Finally, Gracus lowered his goblet and demanded, "But how does my small soldier once again have a straight leg? For I know he limped from it being broken; it was my horse that stepped upon him and I myself set the leg!"

"Now you must indeed believe in miracles," Kaspar told him, and he related the story of the star, the angels, and the wondrous occurrences while He was yet a newborn babe.

"So there is but One God, and not the multitudes I have tried to placate all my life?" Gracus said wonderingly. "And what is the Messiah's given name? Has He one?"

"His parents call Him Jesus of Nazareth," Melchior told Gracus. "You shall hear more of Him in future years."

Before they slept that night, Gracus agreed to escort the three wise men, Thomas, and the caravan back to Tyre.

"My assignment in Zeugma was foreshortened by the emperor," Gracus told them. "He issued orders for many of his soldiers to return to Rome. I go to Tyre myself now to meet the rest of my household." He glanced at Ira, who lay, utterly contented, upon the centurion's bare knees. "I may be involved in some bloody campaigns, once I command the emperor's own troops. This little soldier may have to stay at home to look after Polla and my baby daughter." Ira opened one eye and looked at Gracus, as the other men about the campfire laughed.

Kaspar transferred Ira's basket to Gracus's chariot the next morning, and his foster sisters watched as their brother raised a paw—but with no salute—as he departed, to ride that day in Gracus's chariot once again.

"I hope he doesn't really imagine himself leading the soldiers at the head of the caravan." Kezia giggled.

"Oh, you know Ira," Abishag said. "By now, in his imagination, he's at least a general." Then they leaped into their camels' baskets, setting off on their journey once more, content to know Tyre was the next destination.

Now it was Kezia's turn to peer from her basket, trying to smell the salt air or see the glint of sunshine upon the sea as they traveled closer to Tyre and its enormous harbor.

They entered the city very late at night, and Gracus bid them stay at his temporary home until they could find ships and to see Polla and his baby daughter, Livinia. "She should have been a son," he said, smiling. "But Polla assures me the next will be a son for Caesar."

Two mornings later, the three men and Gracus were on their way to the harbor to secure passage for Balthazar to Antioch, Melchior to Alexandria, and Kaspar to his home in Athens. Melchior had been the object of much teasing, for Kezia set up such a terrible fuss when the men started to leave, he had been compelled to bring her in her basket.

"I do not think it is I from whom she wishes not to part," he grumbled, "for Kaspar has told us often of the snake she killed aboard Alexos's ship, thus saving him from a terrible death. She never killed a snake for me, and yet did I not carry her upon my camel everywhere I went?" And then Melchior laughed.

To Kezia's joy, Alexos's graceful ship *was* in the harbor, and soon a runner was dispatched with a message for him.

The sea captain met them at the same tavern where he and his old friend Gracus had eaten months earlier while settling passage for Gracus's household. The other men didn't tell him of the basket Melchior still carried until they were sitting at a large table awaiting their meal.

"Here, Alexos, a surprise for you," Kaspar said and nodded at Melchior to open the basket.

"It's not a snake, is it?" Alexos asked nervously. He gasped as Kezia leaped from the basket and gracefully landed on the table in front of him.

"My wonder of a cat! The lovely one who saved me from that poisonous snake! Oh, look—how has this happened? Your ear, which I hurt so badly flailing with that trident—your ear is perfectly beautiful once again!" The other men at the table chuckled at Alexos's bewilderment.

Kezia purred so loudly she could be heard over their laughter, and tears stood in Alexos's good eye once again as he stroked her soft fur.

"You are a treasure—and may the gods strike me dead if I am ever parted from you again!"

"Be careful with those vows, Alexos," Kaspar told him. "For I have a wondrous story to relate to you about the One God and His Son the Messiah, Who restored your little cat's ear."

The story told and their meal long finished, Alexos looked at his kinsman. "I have never known you to tell a

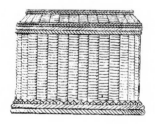

lie," he said to Kaspar. "And so I must turn from my old familiar gods of the seas and thank the Messiah you found—for surely He is the one who restored both my cat's ear and her very presence here to me." The Greek sea captain turned to the tabby, who was still seated upon the table. "I shall get you a silk cushion for your basket; you shall have all the delicacies of the sea that I may coax it into yielding; and you are now and forever the Captain's Cat."

When Abishag saw Kezia the next day, Alexos had fashioned overnight a special collar for her of fishing-net cord, using the smallest sailor's knots he knew. A curiously wrought fish of pure silver hung from the collar.

"Alexos now believes in the old prophecies because of what Kaspar told him yesterday," Kezia explained to her foster sister. She wore the collar her heart's companion had made for her gladly; more proudly than she ever did the topaz stone bracelet Asmodeus had stolen for her. "I am happy to be loved by Alexos and to love my captain in return. The Messiah has brought me home."

Now that just leaves me to have my heart's dearest wish granted, Abishag thought. *I may have my miracle, too!*

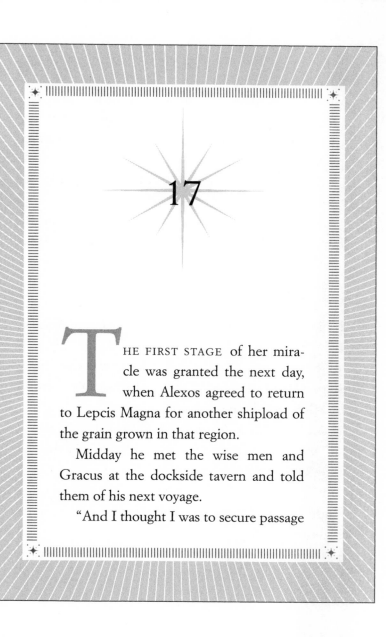

17

THE FIRST STAGE of her miracle was granted the next day, when Alexos agreed to return to Lepcis Magna for another shipload of the grain grown in that region.

Midday he met the wise men and Gracus at the dockside tavern and told them of his next voyage.

"And I thought I was to secure passage

with you to Athens," Kaspar pretended to grumble. "My own ship departed weeks ago, to return to my home. Am I to travel with someone else, as but another passenger?"

"Forgive me, my kinsman, but I must sail where the gold takes me." And Alexos laughed.

Balthazar leaned across the table. "I had nearly forgotten—what of the other small black cat? Who speaks for her? She has not indicated she wishes to remain with any of us."

The men looked at one another, feeling a little guilty because none had realized not one man claimed Abishag as his cat.

"Surely she can sail with her foster sister upon my ship," Alexos decided. "They sailed together before, and they may do so again, and welcome."

And with that, Abishag found herself well started on her trip homeward, as she and Kezia sat by the Greek captain's feet and watched the harbor of Tyre grow ever smaller in the distance and late morning sunshine. They had given Ira their final good-byes the night before they sailed.

It had been a bittersweet farewell; they had endured

much and seen wonders together—and the three cats knew they would never, in all likelihood, see each other again.

They touched noses and slept in their same basket, now quite dilapidated, one last night at Gracus's house. Polla had whispered into each set of furry ears her assurances that they would be most happy with the path they had chosen with their life's companions. And she repeated her prophecy about the five fat kittens she foresaw in her mind's eye, tumbling and playing about Abishag's paws.

Dawn found Ira and Gracus reporting for duty at the garrison, and the wise men were packed and saying their farewells, for each had secured passage home as well. They threw their arms about one another and vowed to send messengers as often as possible to each other.

"For we of the star in our palms have formed an unusual brotherhood," Kaspar said. "And I feel we should keep communication among us, if nothing more than to remind ourselves and each other of the wonders we saw, and the truth of the Messiah being born."

THE VOYAGE TO Lepcis Magna was uneventful; Kezia and Abishag patrolled the ship and kept mice and rats from setting up housekeeping beneath the deck. The weeks flew by almost as fast as the ship skimmed the sea, but it was still far too slow for Abishag. She longed to get her sturdy little legs upon solid ground once again, to begin the final part of her homeward journey.

Then one fine morning Kezia swallowed so hard the small fish on her collar bobbed up and down. "I—I'm going to miss you very much, Abishag," she said. "I look back now and wonder how you and Ira tolerated my foolishness and my overbearing pride."

Abishag smiled at her. "We were all much younger then. And we had not seen the Messiah. He will always bless our lives, of that I am sure."

The two cats said their farewells as Alexos's graceful ship glided to one of the docks in Lepcis Magna.

"I wish you much love, my sister," Kezia said sincerely and touched noses with Abishag.

Abishag looked back as she started to step from the ship's ramp onto the dock. Kezia, looking very small, bravely raised a paw. "Good luck!" she called. "Name one of your kittens after me. Remember—she is to be Kezia the Beautiful!"

Abishag laughed and raised a paw in return. *If I kept my nose pointed toward the North Star to find Lepcis Magna in the first place, then I must keep the tip of my tail pointed to the star to find my way home again. I should have to journey but another week before I am home at last.*

The little black cat retraced the steps she and her foster sister and brother had taken so very long before. *It must be a year, perhaps more. I hope Ptolemy is still alive. And if he is not well, then I shall be home to look after him.*

At dawn of the seventh day, Abishag's heart beat faster as she recognized the old tower, still at a distance.

"May the Messiah grant we have some last happy days together!" she cried and began to run.

She stopped just outside the gate to catch her breath and say a small prayer. *Please, my Messiah, let Ptolemy still be alive, so I may be near him and love him, even if he doesn't love me in the same way.*

She hurried into the dusty courtyard, quiet in the late, fragile sunshine of an early spring day—and saw Ptolemy sitting next to the wall. His muzzle was gray now, not black, and he had white hairs in his tail; but the look upon his face when he saw Abishag made her heart purr.

To her surprise, the elderly astronomer was also still alive, and even had acquired a young assistant, who cheerfully looked after the old man. Abishag happily settled back into the tower quarters with Ptolemy.

He called to her a few days after her return.

"Come and sit in the sunshine with me, and tell me again of the wonders you saw."

The old Siamese walked slowly into the courtyard, sat down, and curled his tail about his paws. Abishag sat next to him and leaned against his shoulder.

"You know that I love you," he said and smiled at her. "But I am far too old for you."

"Nonsense," Abishag replied. "Do you not realize that I love you also?"

"But I will not live to see our kittens grown."

"I will treasure whatever time we have together," Abishag whispered. "I fear you will try to make me leave you, and that alone would break my heart."

Ptolemy sighed and shook his head. "It is terribly selfish of me, my Abishag. But please, stay with me for whatever time I have left upon this earth, for you make my old heart young again." He settled himself to listen, for he wished to hear every detail she could recall of the long journey.

She related the lies and tricks with which Asmodeus had tried to ruin their quest and told him of the chorus of angels and Charko, their guardian angel. When she described again the miraculous gifts the Messiah gave Kezia and Ira in the stable, Ptolemy grew very thoughtful. This time he had a new question.

"And what gift did He give you?" Ptolemy asked gently, his wise old blue eyes studying her saffron golden ones.

"When I looked upon His face, a newborn babe, He reached His hand out to me and touched me. I carry

Him within my heart always," the little black cat said simply.

"So you have not yet seen His gift to you. Come." And Ptolemy led her to the wide pan of water the astronomers used for washing up.

She peeked over the edge of the pan and saw her reflection. Upon her small chest, framed by black fur, was a cross of purest white.